"Elegant." —*Marie Claire*

"Engrossing." —**NBC Latino**

"Fantastic . . . Intense pain and beauty are offset by an unabashedly boyish sense of humor." —**NPR** *Alt.Latino*

"Stimulating and inspiring." —*The Independent*

"A mix of finely nuanced prose and humor."
—*World Literature Today*

"Beautiful and provocative . . . a wonderful read which begs to be re-read." —*Jewish Book World*

"A brave and touching and dead stylish examination of the nature of fiction, truth, and lies." —*Dazed & Confused*

"[*The Polish Boxer*] exists in the no-man's-land between fiction and memoir. In the end, we decide, this is fable: only the stories are important." —*The Guardian*

"A professor mentors a student, gains wisdom from a Mark Twain scholar, and searches for a Gypsy musician, and that's only part of the story in this incredible, achingly real yet enigmatic novel." —*San Francisco Chronicle,* "Top Shelf" Recommendation from Bay Area independent bookstore Copperfield's Books

"[Halfon] has succeeded in warping a modern Balkan mystery into a Holocaust memoir . . . intrinsically blend[ing] fiction with reality in a deeply visceral way." —*The Rumpus*

"A revelation . . . *The Polish Boxer* is a book of small miracles. . . . For sheer narrative momentum and fascination with the mix of life and books, sex and art, there are echoes of the Chilean master Roberto Bolaño."
—*Words Without Borders*

"Halfon passionately and lyrically illustrates the significance of the journey and the beauty of true mystery. *The Polish Boxer* is sublime and arresting, and will linger with readers who will be sure to revisit it again and again." —*Booklist* **(starred review)**

"These are the stories of life . . . the question of survival (of both people and cultures) and the way the fictional makes the real bearable and intelligible."
—*Publishers Weekly* **(boxed review)**

"Brilliant . . . opens with one of the best classroom scenes I've ever read." —*Shelf Awareness*

"Highly readable and engaging . . . provides readers food for thought about the nature of literary creations."
—*Library Journal*

"Eduardo Halfon's prose is as delicate, precise, and ineffable as precocious art—a lighthouse that illuminates everything."
—**Francisco Goldman**, author of *Say Her Name*

"*The Polish Boxer* is the most memorable new novel I have read all year—the voice pitch-perfect, the imagery indelible. What a wonderful writer." —**Norman Lebrecht**, author of *The Song of Names*

"It is not often that one encounters such a mix of personal engagement and literary passion, or pain and tenderness."
—**Andrés Neuman**, author of *Talking to Ourselves* and *Traveler of the Century*

MONASTERY

Eduardo Halfon

Translated by Lisa Dillman
&
Daniel Hahn

BELLEVUE LITERARY PRESS
NEW YORK

First Published in the United States in 2014 by
Bellevue Literary Press, New York

FOR INFORMATION CONTACT:
Bellevue Literary Press
NYU School of Medicine
550 First Avenue
OBV A612
New York, NY 10016

The author and translators would like to thank
the John Simon Guggenheim Memorial Foundation and Ledig House
for their support in the writing and translation of this book.

"The Birds Are Back" was originally commissioned by the Inter-American
Investment Corporation.

An earlier version of "White Sand, Black Stone" was first published by *Words
Without Borders*, November 2013.

Library of Congress Cataloging-in-Publication Data

Halfon, Eduardo, 1971-
[Monasterio. English]
Monastery / by Eduardo Halfon ; translated by Lisa Dillman and Daniel Hahn.—
First edition.
pages cm
ISBN 978-1-934137-82-6 (paperback)—ISBN 978-1-934137-83-3 (ebook)
I. Dillman, Lisa, translator. II. Hahn, Daniel, translator. III. Title.
PQ7499.3.H35M6613 2014
863'.7—dc23
2014025360

Bellevue Literary Press would like to thank all its generous
donors—individuals and foundations—for their support.

This publication is made possible by the New York State Council on
the Arts with the support of Governor Andrew Cuomo and the New
York State Legislature.

Book design and composition by Mulberry Tree Press, Inc.
Manufactured in the United States of America.
FIRST EDITION
1 3 5 7 9 8 6 4 2
paperback ISBN 978-1-934137-82-6
ebook ISBN 978-1-934137-83-3

For my sister, for my brother

A cage went in search of a bird.

—FRANZ KAFKA

MONASTERY

Tel Aviv Was an Inferno

Tel Aviv was an inferno. I never figured out if Ben Gurion Airport simply didn't have air conditioning or if it wasn't working that day or if perhaps someone had decided not to turn it on so that we tourists would acclimate quickly to the sticky Mediterranean heat. My brother and I were standing, exhausted and bleary-eyed, waiting for our bags to come out. It was almost midnight and the airport no longer seemed like an airport. I was surprised to see that several other passengers, also awaiting their bags, lit up cigarettes, so I took one out myself and lit it and the acrid smoke immediately revived me a bit. My brother stole it from me. He let out a smoky sigh that conveyed both rage and indignation and swore under his breath as he wiped his T-shirt sleeve across his forehead. Neither of us wanted to be there, in Tel Aviv, in Israel.

OUR LITTLE SISTER HAD DECIDED to get married. She called us in Guatemala from a pay phone to say she'd met an Orthodox Jew from the United States, or actually that the rabbis at her yeshiva had introduced her to an Orthodox Jew from the United States, from New York, from Brooklyn, and that they'd decided—I never quite understood who, whether the rabbis or the two of them—that they should get married. My father snatched the phone away, shouted for a while, tried to dissuade her for another while, and then, resigned, asked or begged her to wait for us, saying we were on our way.

She'd been living in a women's yeshiva in Jerusalem, studying the Torah and other rabbinical texts, for nearly two years. At first we all thought it was just a touch of Zion fever, or Hebrew fever, or some juvenile obsession with finding a deeper manifestation of our grandparents' religion, and that it would eventually pass. But soon her discourse began to evolve. In letters, in phone calls, her words were no longer her own. Her language, as is always the case with the abruptly devout, became increasingly fierce and flippant, a sermon lacking any tolerance whatsoever. She legally changed her name to the Hebrew version. She began sending us photos in which she appeared—sometimes wearing a head scarf, sometimes a wig—covering up her lovely black curls: according to Orthodox Jewish laws and customs, she explained, a woman's beauty is revealed in her hair, which is a temptation for men, and thus must be hidden. The same with women's skin. My sister, young and beautiful, now wore only long baggy dresses that didn't reveal her shoulders, or her neck, or her arms, and certainly not her legs. As though she were a prisoner of her own attire. As though temptation could actually be concealed beneath a baggy dress and a wig. I remember she came back to Guatemala only once during that time, for a visit. She warned us arrogantly that she could no longer touch any man when she greeted him; that she would prepare her own meals, using two sets of dishes she was bringing from Israel, one for dairy and one for meat; that during the twenty-four hours of Shabbat we were forbidden to drive, work, read, flush any toilets but one (whatever), or turn on any lights barring those that she had strategically left on since sundown the previous Friday and that had to remain on until sundown on Saturday. At some point, I recall, the five of us were sitting around the dining room table at my parents' house, when my sister announced coldly that, as far as she and the Orthodox rabbis and teachers saw it, the four of us were not Jews. My father yelled once or twice. My mother stood and stormed off in tears, and my brother went after her. Well, I replied, at least that's one thing we agree on.

THE BLACK LUGGAGE CAROUSEL still wasn't moving. We'd been waiting for our bags for nearly an hour.

Despite the fact that my brother groused every once in a while, none of the other passengers seemed particularly upset, or particularly surprised. Maybe because we all knew that security measures were tighter in Israel. Maybe because after so many hours in the air, you're just thankful to no longer be crammed into two feet of plane.

How far from here to the hotel? my brother asked. We still had to catch a taxi to Jerusalem. My parents had arrived a few days earlier to deal with who knows what wedding preparations and had told us that when we came out of the airport, we should take a taxi to Hotel Kadima, in Jerusalem, that it was no more than half an hour away, that they'd be waiting for us there. About half an hour, I was about to say to my brother, when suddenly I was dazzled by a fleet of Lufthansa flight attendants. Five or six girls, all wearing radiant Lufthansa uniforms and yellow Lufthansa caps and smiling enormous Lufthansa smiles. We had flown Lufthansa via Frankfurt, where the plane—first while parked at the gate, then during its slow taxi to takeoff—was defended and escorted by two German patrol cars and a military tank.

The five or six flight attendants all headed for a passenger who was leaning up against a huge beer poster, smoking. I felt an immediate pang of guilt. I crushed my cigarette out on the floor. The man—maybe fifty, bald, fat, pale, sweaty, in shorts and rubber sandals—showed them his passport and ticket as he began arguing loudly, in Hebrew or Arabic. One of the girls held the man's documents and, judging by her face and gestures, seemed to be telling him to accompany them someplace. But the man just shouted louder and louder. Two soldiers, dressed in green and toting machine guns, appeared out of nowhere and stationed themselves on either side of the man. One of the soldiers was insisting the man surrender his backpack, but the man clasped it tightly to his chest and appeared to be shouting that he'd never give it up alive, or at least not without a good fight. The black carousel had begun to turn; the first bags were coming out. Not one of the passengers cared. We all stared at the man with curiosity and fear and a touch of expectation. Several passengers even approached, out of nosiness, just in case, to help or to lend the flight attendants their support if need be. But suddenly, in what was clearly an expert and premeditated move, the two soldiers grabbed the man, threw him to the ground, cuffed him, and dragged him off as he continued shouting in Hebrew or Arabic. That easy. That quick.

Several of the Lufthansa flight attendants then left as well. But two of them stood in the same spot, whispering among themselves and calming down several of the passengers. My brother looked at me, gaping, eyes wide open, shaking his head slowly. Perhaps thinking: Nice welcome. Or perhaps thinking: Where the fuck have we landed? I shrugged.

We walked slowly back to the carousel, which was creaking and screeching, but creaking and screeching with poise, with grace, like a grandiose relic of some sort. I don't know why I turned once more to look back at the two Lufthansa flight attendants. Nor do I know why—although I assume the yellow gleam of the uniform had something to do with it—it took me so long to recognize her.

It can't be, I said to my brother, excited, grabbing onto his arm. What? he asked. Look, I said. Look at what? There, the flight attendant, I said, signaling with my eyes. I think it's her, I said. Think it's who? Perhaps he was still dazzled by the yellow Lufthansa uniforms, or he didn't recognize her, or he'd never actually met her and I'd only told him about her. The flight attendant, I said, signaling with my eyes again. Yeah, I see her, what about her? I let go of his arm and stood staring at her for a few seconds, doubting, or maybe fearful. I think it's Tamara, I said. Who? Tamara, I repeated, a bit surprised to have remembered her name after so long, a name that now sounded sublime, foreign, fictional even.

My brother gazed at her for a few seconds, struggling to rewind the years, to recall, to place himself in the past and sift through all those dusty images. That's crazy, he said, impossible. How could it be her? It's her, I said, studying her eyes and her lips and her pale freckled cheeks and her copper hair streaked with gray.

Her hair's shorter and grayer now, but that's Tamara, I said, nearly convinced and starting slowly in her direction. Wait, where are you going? my brother said from behind me, the bags are starting to come out. Could it be her? Could it really be Tamara? Would she recognize me after all those years? Would she remember me? Would she hug me or kiss me or maybe even slap me? Don't do it, my brother shouted over the creaking carousel, it's not her.

Tamara? I said, touching her shoulder.

It was one in the morning when my brother and I finally stepped onto the sidewalk outside the airport. There were multiple taxis, from multiple companies, in multiple colors. Without much thought, we approached a red-and-white minivan that looked a bit more official and said to the driver: Hotel Kadima, in Jerusalem. The guy, looking angry and harried and motioning to the back, said yes, yes, Kadima, Yerushalayim. We opened the minivan's rear doors, stashed our bags, walked back around, and got in through the side door. In the first row sat a couple of French tourists who I assumed were also going to Hotel Kadima in Jerusalem. We said hello, taking our seats behind them in the second row, exhausted.

So? my brother asked again, impatient. The taxi driver was shouting at someone over the radio. I began to find it odd that he didn't close his door, didn't start the engine so we could get moving. Are you going to tell me or not? my brother asked, his eyes half-closed and his tone confrontational. I leaned back against the headrest. Scarlet, I told him.

Before I saw her timid smile, before I saw her blue Mediterranean eyes widen, I knew Tamara finally recognized me as soon as I saw the minuscule freckles on her cheeks disappear in a sudden scarlet flush. But from then on, it was all awkward. We hugged awkwardly. We asked and answered each other's questions awkwardly, with clichés, with the animated chaos and apprehension that came of having our little reunion in public, amid all the passengers and the suitcases and the stifling heat of the airport and the obvious gravity of her Lufthansa uniform, interrupting each other and stumbling over each other in an attempt to sum up all those years in a few seconds. Then we fell silent awkwardly, each of us perhaps thinking of a brief and distant encounter we thought we'd left behind but which was suddenly back and erupting with the force of a volcano. She asked me in English how long I was going to be in Israel, and I stammered and said a few days, just a few days, just for my little sister's wedding, and yes, an Orthodox wedding, and yes, in Jerusalem, and yes, at Hotel Kadima. Her Lufthansa colleague called her, as if to hurry her up, and Tamara said something to her in Hebrew. Then she took out a scrap of paper and scribbled down her phone number and said that I should call her, that she lived very close to Hotel Kadima, that she could pick me up and take me to see some sights. Okay, Eduardo? she asked, pronouncing my name as though it weren't my name or as though it were a version of my name that was hers alone, and sending me back to a Scottish bar and a few beers and a heart-shaped mouth and nipples that were to be bitten hard or soft, it all depended. Okay? she said again, and leaned close. She handed me the slip of paper. She pressed her freckled scarlet cheek to mine and left it there. Please do call, she whispered, now not awkwardly at all and in a tone that conveyed much more than those three words. I liked the contrast of her warm breath and her cold cheek. I liked that I recognized her scent. I folded the slip of paper and stuck it into my shirt pocket. Will you call? she asked, and took a few steps backward. Absolutely, I said, this time I will. You can count on it, and I gave her a slight smile, and then Tamara said something in Hebrew, perhaps good-bye, perhaps you'd better, and walked off with her Lufthansa colleague.

So will you call? asked my brother, who for over an hour had been dozing off and on and cursing me, the taxi driver, the military detritus left like decor all along the highway, the French tourists, the labyrinthine and never-ending nocturnal odyssey to our Jerusalem hotel. I don't know, I said shaking my head in vain into the darkness of a minivan now with no other passengers.

One of the five previous passengers, a young Israeli returning from Peru, had explained to us in Spanish that this was a collective taxi, called a sherut. I fell silent, recalling Tamara's flushed face, recalling Tamara's lavender scent, and recalling with a start the white gold on her left ring finger.

Had she been wearing a white-gold ring? Had I, in fact, seen it, or was I imagining it now, in the silence of an empty minivan? Had she gotten married?

When we finally pulled up in front of the hotel, it was three in the morning.

I ALWAYS SLEEP POORLY IN HOTELS. I had asked the receptionist, as I usually do, for a room on the top floor, one that wasn't overlooking the noisy street, as far as possible from the elevator, with no inner door connecting it to an adjoining room. But whether by mistake or misunderstanding, the curmudgeonly old man informed us in his abominable English that he had only one room available, with a king-size bed. We were both too tired to protest. We just took the key in silence and rode up in the tiny, rickety old elevator.

Everything in the room looked filthy and run-down: the bathroom, the sheets, the muted carpet covered in mysterious stains, the olive green muslin curtains. Before going to bed, I unplugged the television, turned off the alarm on the bedside table, and covered every crack and strip of light (I always travel with a roll of masking tape). And still, lying next to my brother, I slept poorly. At some point in the night, I was awakened by shrieking or wailing, like a baby crying or a woman mid-orgasm. I couldn't tell if it was coming from out-side or from a neighboring room or if perhaps I had dreamed it. At noon, I finally bathed and dressed—my brother was sleeping soundly—and went down to the lobby for breakfast.

The restaurant was empty. The elderly receptionist appeared, the same one who had been at the front desk at three in the morning and had put up with my neu-roses and appeals for a silent room. He looked awful. More sleep-deprived than I. His wrinkled white shirt, dirty and half-tucked; his face, greenish and unshaven; his few remaining strands of black hair (fake black, excessive black, shoe polish black), spit-stuck to his balding pate. He told me in English that they only served breakfast until eleven. I simply stared at him, as though I hadn't understood, and he sighed and told me to take a seat, that he'd try to find me something in the kitchen. His kindness surprised me, perhaps because he said everything gruffly and with a sour expression. I smiled at him. Coffee? he asked. Yes, thank you. How kind, thank you. Black, thank you. I took a seat at the table closest to the entrance.

I was a bit disappointed to note that nothing in there looked like Israel. It could have been any restaurant, in any hotel. It had the same decorations and furniture and maybe even the same background music as any other cheap hotel. I don't know why—maybe because I was still half-asleep, maybe because I'm an idiot—I'd been expecting a sandy floor and enormous walls made of biblical clay. The elderly receptionist returned. Without a word, he set down first a large tray holding pita bread, green olives, cubes of feta, slices of tomato and cucumber, and then a strange coffee cup. I wanted to ask him how the thing worked, what kind of magic I had to perform in order to drink from it, but he'd already shambled off, muttering under his breath. I studied the red plastic contraption and it slowly dawned on me that resting atop the cup was a individual filter—for lack of a better term—full of hot water and ground coffee, and that my individual filter was slowly draining and just-brewed coffee was dripping down into my cup. I waited patiently and possibly with a smile until the cup filled. I removed the plastic filter and set it on the table-cloth. Perhaps because it was so novel, perhaps because the engineer in me is still awed by this sort of device, that first cup of Israeli coffee tasted exquisite. I drank it slowly, experiencing a sense of well-being or optimism, and thinking of Tamara.

IT OCCURRED TO ME that I should get out of the hotel and take a stroll, stretch my legs, maybe smoke a cigarette. As I walked through the lobby, the same elderly receptionist motioned to me. He handed me a yellow slip of paper. It was standard stationery, a stock memo, and contained a note written in my mother's handwriting (all caps): They'd be out all day shopping and getting things ready for the wedding, and we'd all meet that night for dinner. I thought about calling up to the room to wake my brother up and tell him. But all I did was hand the note back to the elderly receptionist, thank him, and walk out of the hotel.

The bright daylight hurt my eyes. Undecided, I spent some time staring at the traffic, at shop windows, at pedestrians rushing anxiously. I saw a taxi driver sitting in his taxi, reading the paper. I walked over and asked him in English if he could take me to the Jerusalem market—the first place that occurred to me. He put his paper aside and started the engine.

He was wearing a khaki cap, a fisherman's cap. His radio was on too loud, tuned to the news or maybe a debate in Hebrew, and as he drove, he kept stealing glances at me in the rearview mirror. Suddenly he shouted in acceptable English, asking where I was from. Guatemala, I told him. I don't know if he didn't hear or didn't understand or didn't care. But Jewish? he shouted, almost insolently. I smiled and said: Sometimes. What do you mean, sometimes? his eyes squinting, his question abusive, his voice abrasive and obstructed, as though he were talking with a mouthful of grapes. I didn't feel like explaining such a bad joke. I just asked if I could smoke a cigarette. Yes, good, cigarette, he said, still inspecting me in the rearview mirror. I had only one Guatemalan cigarette left. Arab? he asked, and I said no. Bad people, Arabs, he proclaimed in his deficient English over the shouting on the news and the sound of the wind rushing in from the window. I stared at the back of his neck: fat, sweaty, crimson. I was going to tell him that my grandfather had been an Arab Jew from Beirut, and my grandmother an Arab Jew from Alexandria, and my other grandmother an Arab Jew from Aleppo, and so that made me a little Arab too—three parts Arab, in fact, one part Polish—but instead I sat staring at the back of his sun-scorched neck and toying with my last cigarette but not lighting it. Bad people, Arabs, he said again. Very bad. We have to kill them, he said, eyeing me in the rearview mirror. He slammed on the brakes for a red light. Look at that, the taxi driver said. Stepping out in front of us, amid a group of people crossing the street, was a woman in a black burka leading a girl of five or six by the hand. Filthy people, he said. We must kill the Arabs, he shouted again into the rearview mirror. You don't think? he asked, observing me, perhaps challenging me. His eyes in the mirror suddenly looked black, empty, lifeless, like fake doll eyes. You're right, I said into his black eyes, we have to kill them all. His black eyes finally smiled a bit. But how should we do it? I inquired. Eh? he grunted, his eyes flitting in the rear-view mirror. What method do you propose we use to kill them? I asked bluntly, and the man fell silent, perplexed or perhaps aggravated, and I swallowed bile.

My derisive reaction surprised me. I was more upset with myself than with the man and his ignorance and his stupid homily of hatred for the Arabs. I wondered how many Israelis thought like he did. I wondered how many Jews thought like he did. I decided it was best not to know.

The taxi driver sped up and careered through the narrow streets of Jerusalem—a word, I recalled bitterly, that meant city of peace.

It took me a while to notice that the cigarette was crumpled in my fist.

Let me out here, I told him, although I had no idea where we were. The man spat something back at me in Hebrew, and I simply repeated, unrelenting: Let me out here. He braked violently, pulling over to one side of the street. I tossed my cigarette debris onto the floor of his taxi and handed him a few dollars and left him there talking to himself, perhaps insulting me, perhaps offering me my change.

THE WIND BLEW SOFT AND HUMID. It was hot. I walked all over, half-lost, among people who seemed to be on the same slow pilgrimage. I couldn't get rid of a metallic taste in my mouth. I couldn't stop thinking about the taxi driver, his black eyes, his fat sweaty neck, his contemptuous words. I couldn't stop thinking about my Arab grandparents, my three parts Arab.

THINKING ABOUT MY maternal grandmother. Her Syrian parents fled Aleppo and made it to America and, thanks to an itinerant life of card playing (my great-grandfather, a compulsive gambler, had squandered all the family's money on poker and bets), their children were born in Mexico, in Panama, in Cuba, in Guatemala. My grandmother often told me that her Syrian father allowed his children only to kiss his hand. That's it. Just his hand. As though he were a mighty sheik, bedecked, bejeweled, smoking a golden hookah. My father died, she once told me, and I never once got to hug him.

THINKING ABOUT MY paternal grandfather. From Lebanon. He and his seven brothers and sisters had fled Beirut at the turn of the twentieth century (my great-grandmother died during their escape and was buried in some Jewish cemetery in Corsica). Curiously, employing what might have been some commercial survival strategy, they decided that each brother and sister would settle in a different city: in Paris, in Guatemala City, in Mexico City, in Cali, in Lima, in Havana, in Manhattan, in Miami (the great-uncle I remember best—handsome, an opera singer, friend or member of Miami's Italian Mafia—served time in a Florida jail for being a gigolo). My Lebanese grandfather, after spending a few years in Paris, was the one who then saved his brother in Guatemala from bankruptcy. That was where he met my grandmother. That was where he opened a store in El Portal del Comercio. That was where he built his palace.

THINKING ABOUT MY paternal grandmother. Born in Alexandria, Egypt. With her parents and sisters, she set sail from Egypt at the age of seven. The ship, after several months on the high seas, finally docked at the first port in Central America, and according to family legend, my great-grandfather thought they'd arrived in Panama, where one of his distant cousins lived. There they disembarked. And there they stayed. In Guatemala. By accident.

I'D BEEN WANDERING for a couple of hours through who knows what heaving streets and alleyways. The walking, or the sweat, or the nostalgia, or simply the time elapsed, calmed me down a bit. I exchanged dollars for shekels at a kiosk. I needed cigarettes. I was thirsty. I walked into a corner bazaar, dark and dingy, a sort of general store. An Israeli teenager, a girl of maybe seventeen or eighteen, sold me a pack of cigarettes and a very cold beer, and I took a long swallow right there at the counter, standing before her. She had beautiful, marked features—large dark eyes, thick brows, very black hair, prominent nose, taut young skin with a soft olive tone. She had a round greenish tattoo on her shoulder. All of a sudden, she moved her right hand just above the bulb of a small rustic lamp on the counter and starting making animal shadows on the ceiling. Each time she made a new shadow, she whispered a word in Hebrew. The name of each animal, I supposed. She might have made a dog, and a swan, and a horse, and a crocodile. I finished my beer in silence, watching her small hand play in the amber light of the bulb. Then I thanked her in Hebrew and said good-bye in Hebrew and she mocked my Hebrew pronunciation with a pretty smile, while up on the ceiling the shadow of her hand said good-bye. Sometimes it's easy to confuse youth for beauty.

I walked on. Down narrow dusty streets, down wide commercial avenues, past fig and date sellers and shawarma sellers and falafel sellers, past too many shops selling too much crap for too many tourists. After a while I came to some steps leading down to an enormous bustling plaza, full of people all congregated in one corner. I recognized the Wailing Wall. The Kotel, in Hebrew. I felt a touch of vertigo and sat on a step to contemplate the swarming plaza.

I lit a cigarette. As I smoked, I tried to remember the story of that remnant of wall, so solemn and biblical, that final vestige of the Temple of the Jews, of my ancestors. But all I could remember was the song by the Cure.

Standing there, still humming the tune of Robert Smith's flute, I stubbed out my cigarette on the clay step and made my way down.

Instantly, I was besieged by Orthodox Jews in long black robes and black suits and black skullcaps. Rabbis maybe. They grabbed my arm and tugged on me and offered me who knows what in Hebrew and in English. One after the other. Stalking me. Circling me, like the buzzards in the song. I passed a guy on his knees. I passed another guy who seemed to be shouting at the entire city, with rage, and maybe even tears, and in Baptist-sounding English, with a thick Southern accent. Widow, he shouted at Jerusalem. Slave, he shouted at her. Tributary, he shouted at her. You lie there alone amid so many people, he shouted at her with ever more rage but now eyeing me, as though I were the one to blame for his anguish, and so I hurried through the rabbis and preachers and tourists and soldiers and finally I reached the wall. I saw people praying aloud, or in silence, or as they swayed, or hidden beneath huge white shawls (tallit, in Hebrew), with small black boxes on their foreheads and black straps wound around their forearms (tefillin, in Hebrew). I saw people taking pictures of the wall, and people kissing it, and people tucking little folded-up slips of paper into its cracks and crevices. I saw vegetation sprouting all along the wall: dry, scrawny, miserable. It struck me, taking it all in, that never had a wall's name been more fitting.

I approached. I reached out inconspicuously, cautiously, as though I were doing something forbidden, and I touched it. I wanted to feel something, anything. All I felt was stone.

ON A DIFFERENT TRIP, to a different city, bundled up in a woman's pink coat, I had also touched the last remnants of what had once been the wall of the Warsaw ghetto. One last redbrick wall between two buildings in Warsaw, between Sienna Street and Zlota Street. It was perhaps six or seven feet tall and thirty feet long. I touched it several times, from several angles, at both ends, with both hands. And I didn't feel anything there either. Or maybe I refused to feel anything. But then suddenly, when I got even closer, I saw that many of the bricks had something engraved in their red clay, like a bas-relief. The same engraving in bas-relief: a sort of small circle with two numbers—a 10 and a 1—separated by a diagonal slash. It occurred to me, stroking it with my finger, that it might be the emblem of the brick company, that it might be the logo of the company that had been contracted to manufacture all the bricks for the wall of the ghetto, to manufacture thousands and thousands of bricks that would imprison an entire people for years, until they'd been eliminated from the city, until they'd been starved to death. I kept stroking the logo with my finger. I imagined factory workers unknowingly producing brick after brick with that same logo in bas-relief, tattooing it in bas-relief: their broad backs, their burly arms, their faces filthy and sweaty, their hands stained forever red.

I WAS ABOUT TO LEAVE the Wailing Wall, when I saw on the ground, under my foot, a dirty white slip of folded paper. I crouched down, picked it up, brushed it off, and unfolded it. It was in Hebrew. It was a single sentence, short, black, written in Hebrew letters. I recognized two or three. I remembered how pointless my Hebrew classes had been as a boy—just memorizing the sounds of vowels and consonants—before I turned thirteen. It occurred to me that it was probably someone's prayer, and that it had also probably fallen from a crack in the wall. I folded it back up. And I don't know why, but moving quickly, almost fleeing, almost running away from something or someone, I slipped it into my pants pocket.

OF THE BIRDS YOU SHALL HAVE in abomination, and shall not be eaten, are the following.

My sister's fiancé, in black jacket and white shirt, paused.

I put down the huge menu. I watched him, his forehead aimed upward as if posing, or as if concentrating, or as if searching there for the words from the Torah he was reciting from memory. I thought his little black skullcap was about to fall to the floor.

Brooklyn. That's where he told us he was from, as soon as he sat down. Born and raised in Brooklyn. His father, he told us, was a driver in Brooklyn. Limo driver, he told us. His mother worked in a beauty salon in Brooklyn. They were divorced. Didn't speak to each other. Weren't even Orthodox. Never went to temple. It had been years since he'd heard a word from his only sister. He said he was in Alcoholics Anonymous, that he liked to tell people that up front, from the outset, right off the bat. No reason to hide it. That's who he was. No one in his family, he told us, would be attending the wedding.

The eagle, the vulture, the osprey, he commenced in slow enumeration.

He paused again. He was still gazing upward, eyes fixed on the ceiling. His little black skullcap was holding tight. It was fastened to his straight brown hair with a metal bobby pin.

The kite, he went on, the falcon according to its kind, every raven according to its kind, the ostrich, the nighthawk, the seagull, the hawk according to its kind, the owl, the cormorant, the ibis, the water hen, the pelican, the carrion vulture, the stork, the heron according to its kind, the hoopoe, and the bat.

He finally looked down. Smiled at me. As he was taking a sip of water, proud of himself and his verbatim memorization of the Torah, I informed him that the bat wasn't a bird. I heard him swallow, hard. That is how it is written, he scolded me, wiping his lips with the back of his hand. The bat is a mammal, I told him. That is how it is written in Leviticus, he repeated, ignoring me, barricading himself behind the ever-literal interpretation of zealots. It flies, I told him. It looks like a bird, but it's not a bird. It says in Leviticus, he told me, that those are the birds you shall have in abomination, and shall not be eaten. Silence. Now, in the Mishnah, he went on, it says that birds of prey are not kosher, because to be kosher a bird must possess three characteristics. There is one species of bat, I interrupted his exegesis before he could enumerate the three characteristics, that hibernates for six months in coitus. In what? asked my mother. In coitus, six months, I declared, picking the huge menu back up (my own barricade). That's not right, my brother corrected. What it is, he explained, is that this particular species of bat reproduces only while hibernating, a state that lasts six months and in which the males mate with several other hibernating bats, half-asleep, who don't even know what's going on. He smiled. Some of which, he said smiling wider, are also males. Thirty-five percent of them are males, I chimed in. That's right—he winked—thirty-five percent of the males mate with other males. More silence.

We'd watched a documentary on bats when I got back to the hotel room that evening, sitting on the narrow balcony and sharing a cigarette my brother had expertly rolled, and which my father, who came to pick us up and show us his new baseball cap (FATHER OF THE BRIDE, in gold letters), had thought was a joint.

Right, I said to my brother, just to keep it going, but I prefer to believe that a single act of coitus can last six months. What are you talking about? asked my father, as though he'd just awakened, his new cap still on, still stiff. Myotis lucifugus, I said. Long acts of coitus, I said. Bisexual bats, my brother said. We both smiled. What on earth are you talking about? my mother asked impatiently, near exasperation. I knew it was marijuana, my father said, half-joking and half-gullible. I was surprised that my sister, beneath her wig and hat (her own barricade), sat judging us only with her eyes, not saying a word. My sister's fiancé raised a hand, requesting the floor once more. At any rate, according to law, you are allowed to eat duck, he granted me, his tone pious, his hand held out priestlike. I was about to thank him for his gracious consent. Fortunately, the waiter arrived.

My mother, perhaps in an attempt not to cry, simply kept taking quick sips of her heavily sugared green tea.

My sister and her fiancé announced that, although it was supposedly a kosher restaurant, they wouldn't eat anything in a place like this, saying these last two words with special emphasis, italicizing them. Disdainful and standoffish, whispering to each other—no touching till after the wedding—they drank only water. My father and brother shared a huge plate of vegetable chow mein in silence. My Peking duck was dry and overcooked.

I FELT MY BROTHER KICK my leg and edged farther away from him and, faceup in our king-size bed, forced myself to recall those six words.

As kids, my brother and I slept in the same room, our beds arranged perpendicularly, head-to-head. Every night after we brushed our teeth and got under the covers, my mother would finally come in, pick up our clothes, tidy up a few toys strewn on the floor, and ask us: Have you said your prayer yet? Then each of us, tucked under the covers, would repeat those six words in Hebrew, always the same prayer in Hebrew—quick, perfunctory, rote. First word: Shema. Second word: Yisrael. Third word: Adonai. Fourth word: Eloheinu. Fifth word: Adonai. Sixth word: Echad. Six words. The same six words in Hebrew that made no sense to us, that had no meaning beyond invoking the presence of my mother, who would come in to say good-night, to kiss us good-night. We would each mumble those six words and then get a kiss on the forehead and then we could fall asleep. Life was simple. Sleep was sweet. Prayers, perfunctory or not, comprehensible or not, made their own kind of sense. I can't imagine a prayer, any prayer, having a meaning more profound than a mother's good-night kiss. I don't remember when we stopped saying that prayer, my brother and I. Maybe during the cynicism of adolescence. Maybe when we each got our own room. Maybe when my mother stopped offering a good-night kiss in exchange for those six words, and those six words definitively lost all their meaning, all their logic.

I felt my brother's cold feet on mine as he lay beside me in a deep and peaceful slumber. Perhaps to get back at him, or to make sure I could actually remember them, or to see if they still held any enchanted maternal sway, I began whispering those six words into the darkness of the night, lying faceup, exhaling them up, using all of my breath to drive them upward. Over, and over, and over. Until the six words became a flat shapeless mass and I got bored or maybe I just fell asleep.

I'm giving that asshole ten more minutes.

My brother, furious, was sitting on the sidewalk beneath the meager shade of a cypress, rolling another cigarette. I kept quiet. I know his fury well, and the best thing to do is keep quiet. We'd been waiting almost an hour at the entrance to a Jerusalem neighborhood called Kiryat Mattersdorf.

The night before, as we left the Chinese restaurant, my sister had asked us to meet her fiancé there, at the main entrance, on Panim Meirot Street. He wanted to show us around the neighborhood of the yeshiva where he studied. My brother and I immediately smiled at each other, each with the same thought: Not a chance. We said no thank you, and my sister shook her head in disgust and said she didn't even know why we had come, then mumbled something that might have been in Hebrew, turned, and stormed off. But the next morning (again I'd heard or dreamed the same shrieking or wailing in the night), my mother came to the room to wake us up: her face forlorn, her voice desperate, pleading that we go, that it wasn't much to ask, that it would be for only a short while, that it was for our sister's sake, for our brother-in-law's sake. She called him that. Our brother-in-law. I hadn't thought of him as a brother-in-law. There are words that suddenly lose all meaning.

TWO VERY YOUNG SOLDIERS passed by, holding machine guns, dressed in green, wearing black berets, and on seeing them, possibly because I was tired of waiting, I instantly recalled the one time I'd played in a heavy-metal concert. I was fifteen or sixteen. The band had telephoned me because they urgently needed a keyboardist for a concert that weekend, and they knew I played piano. They were punk, or heavy metal, or some bizarre mix of the two. They were called, to my parents' horror, Crucifix. I didn't understand their urgency. I didn't understand what piano had to do with heavy metal. And though I didn't like that kind of music at all, flattered and naïve, I accepted. We practiced once or twice at the singer's house, and it took me no time to learn the simple, repetitive, monotonous chords of their songs. I showed up the day of the concert in jeans and a button-down shirt and they laughed at my preppy attire, and with leather and chains and black makeup and black boots and a black beret, they proceeded to disguise me as a punk rocker. We played to a theater full of teenagers, and I tickled a few keys here and there. When I got back home, I was still euphoric. Maybe even humming one of their metallic melodies. I went into the bathroom and turned on the light and contemplated the punk rocker in the mirror. My costume, I suppose, had worked. I wet a towel and leaned in toward the mirror to take the makeup off my eyes, only to discover that on the black beret, smack-dab in the middle of my forehead, was an enormous swastika. A Nazi swastika. I snatched the cap off my head to inspect it from up close, without the distortion of the mirror. The swastika was embroidered in black thread. Factory stitching, expert stitching. I remembered that as they were dressing me, someone had hurriedly stuck the beret on my head. I never saw it, never saw myself with the beret on, never knew that I'd played two hours to a full audience dressed as a Nazi punk rocker. Did that make me a Nazi, at least for those two hours, at least in the eyes of those teenagers? I felt something in my stomach. Nausea, maybe. It was already after midnight, but I went back out. I walked for blocks, until I'd gotten far enough away from my house. I came to a wasteland and cast the beret into some bushes, hard, far, as if casting into the night my honor or my guilt.

HERE HE COMES, I said to my brother, eyeing my sister's fiancé as he crossed the street toward us, his gait slow and disdainful. He was still wearing the same black suit and the same white shirt as the night before. You can't smoke once we go in, he said the moment he approached us, no greeting whatsoever, no apology whatsoever for his late arrival. My brother muttered something, stood up, and wearing an expression I knew all too well, continued to smoke his cigarette in a leisurely fashion, making us stand there waiting until he'd finished the whole thing.

As we walked to the entrance, my sister's fiancé explained that the neighborhood of Kiryat Mattersdorf was Haredi, perhaps the most conservative offshoot of Orthodox Judaism, also known as ultra-Orthodox. He was telling us something or other about the rabbi who'd founded it in 1959, when we passed a big security gate, painted bright yellow, still open. What's this for? I asked, interrupting him. To close the street off later, he said, for Shabbos (the Yiddish word for Shabbat). I asked him why. He said it was forbidden for cars to come through during Shabbos. He said driving a car on Shabbos was forbidden. He said that this law was based on one of the thirty-nine prohibitions of the Mishnah, the first text written about Jewish oral traditions. He said a Jew never questions what is written in sacred texts, as they are the laws of Hashem, who is all-powerful. He said that since today was Friday, there was a lot going on. Shabbos is almost upon us, he said. We're preparing for Shabbos, which begins in less than an hour, he said, his eyes raised heavenward.

In a tour-guide voice, and in something of a rush, he showed us the outside of the building where his yeshiva was located. He showed us the building that was the synagogue, and the building that was the school, and the building that was the old people's home. We kept walking down the street and he kept pointing out buildings where some famous rabbi or other lived, and where yet another famous rabbi or other lived, saying their names as if we knew who they were or as if we cared. He introduced us to several of his friends, all dressed like him and all speaking like him and almost all American. The women, wearing the same dresses and head scarves as my sister, ignored us. The Orthodox kids laughed and played around us the way all kids laugh and play.

My brother wasn't saying anything. From time to time, we simply turned to look at each other or glanced at our watches or shook our heads. I felt as though we'd suddenly stepped into another country. A country radically different from the one we'd left a few steps behind, just on the other side of the yellow security gate. A country physically confined, decidedly self-contained, cloistered somewhere between yellow security gates and huge invisible walls.

I noticed many of the men heading for the same door of an old cream-colored building. All of a sudden, we too were heading for the door of that old cream-colored building. We walked up dark steps to the fourth floor, the highest floor, and for the first time that afternoon I felt nervous.

THE APARTMENT SMELLED of sweat, of taffeta, of confined bodies. The front door was left open and black-suited men came and went. Some wore lightweight black overcoats. Some wore black felt hats. Some wore straggly beards, while others wore them neat and trimmed. Some greeted us with a pompous gesture or whispered at us in Hebrew or possibly in Yiddish. We went through the entryway and through the dining room and a long hallway and came to a room full of men standing and sitting on sofas and folding chairs. Maybe twenty or thirty men, all dressed in black, all praying. Not a single woman. Looking toward the back, I caught sight of a great white mound atop an armchair that more resembled a throne. White cloth. White silk or satin. I got the impression that all of the men there were praying to the great white mound. It took me a while to realize that within the white mound, like a shelled seed poking out from the center of it, was a head.

Rabbi Scheinberg, my sister's fiancé whispered to us. Who? I asked. Deliberate, disgruntled, he replied: Rabbi Chaim Pinchas Scheinberg. Who's that? I asked, watching the tiny round head covered in gray hair, and my sister's fiancé adopted a solemn air and exhaled a slight puff of air to make my ignorance clear. A great rabbi, he said. Rosh yeshiva, he said. Morei d'asra, he said. Posek, he said. Gadol hador, he said. And all I got was that he was an important old man, well respected in the community. Right, I said, suddenly realizing that what was on top of the old man were dozens, maybe hundreds, of white shawls, white tallit. Why's he like that? I whispered to my sister's fiancé. Like what? Like that, I said, hiding, practically buried under all those tallit. Tales, he corrected me, using the Yiddish rather than the Hebrew word. I knew little about what the white shawls—tallit or tales or whatever they were called—signified to Jews, beyond the fact that men wore them during prayer, on their shoulders and sometimes on their heads, like some sort of scarf or tunic. I remembered the one I'd had as a boy, all white, with sky blue and gold lines. I remembered its maroon suede case. I remembered one time when I dropped it mid-prayer in the Sephardic synagogue (there were two synagogues in Guatemala: an old Sephardic one in the center of the city, and a newer Ashkenazi one built in the shape of a Star of David and right next to a McDonald's), and my father rebuked me as though I'd just broken a very precious object and then made me pick it up off the floor and kiss it. My sister's fiancé, in hushed tones, explained to us that Rabbi Scheinberg was the only rabbi in the world to wear so many tales at once. Why does he do it? I asked, whispering. My sister's fiancé smiled with condescension. Perhaps he welcomed my question. There are many different opinions among rabbis about how the tales should be worn, he said, and how the tzitzit should be tied. What's that? Tzitzit, he said, are the knotted strands at the end of the tales. These, he said, showing me his. Right, I muttered. Rabbi Scheinberg, he said, wishes to respect all the different views on how to wear a tales and how to tie a tzitzit, and that's why he wears so many tales when he prays, he explained, all those tales, a tales for each view. He fell silent and I kept staring at the old man's pale little head. He looked as though he were in need of air. He looked as though he were suffocating. He looked as though he were drowning in all that cloth. He looked as though he were being buried beneath that which should have saved him. I felt pity, and fear, and perhaps a certain humility. Suddenly, my brother, who had said nothing up to that point, whispered: So what you're saying is that rather than take a stand, he wants to get in good with everybody at the same time. But my sister's fiancé either didn't hear him or decided to ignore him. This is a privilege for you, he said. I wanted you to experience this. This is my gift to you. I'm going to stay and pray, but you two can go, he said, and he was swallowed up by the black sea of men.

Outside, it was beginning to get dark. The yellow security gate was down. A festive air prevailed in Kiryat Mattersdorf, in the buildings, in the houses and apartments, in the entire neighborhood. But not in the two of us.

We walked in silence out to Panim Meirot, the main street, and began waiting for a taxi. All of a sudden, without giving it much thought, not sure if I was serious, I told my brother I wasn't going to the wedding. A taxi sped by without stopping. Then another one. What do you mean you're not going to the wedding? Exactly that, I said, I'm not going to the wedding. And why not? he asked. I didn't know how to respond, how to explain the exasperation I was feeling toward all that pretentiousness, all that farce. Or was it fear I felt? Was it something else? What was I actually trying to escape from? I didn't know. The only thing I did know was that I needed to get as far away as possible from all of that, and from all of them, and maybe, if I could, even from myself. I don't know, I whispered to my brother, and he frowned and shook his head and said, raising his voice, that we were there for our sister, that it was our sister's wedding, that the wedding was what we'd come to Israel for, that I was crazy. Yeah, could be, but I'm not going. I can't. Another taxi sped by. You can't or you don't want to? my brother asked, his voice now rather aggressive. I exhaled and replied, my voice just as aggressive, that it was the same shit. Because of all this, I suppose? he asked, almost as though it were an insult, his fiery glance cast back, perhaps encompassing all of the buildings of Kiryat Mattersdorf, perhaps encompassing all of Judaism. Maybe, I said. Well if that's the case, he said, then you're being more intolerant than they are. I kept quiet. Whether you like it or not, he said, whether you accept it or not, you're as Jewish as all of them. That's the way it is. That's your heritage. It's in your blood.

It struck me then, watching my brother stand there in front of all of the gray buildings of Kiryat Mattersdorf, that the discourse about Judaism being in the blood, the discourse about Judaism not being a religion but something genetic, sounded the same as the discourse used by Hitler.

There are thoughts that jump up, dark and clammy, like little frogs.

Neither of us spoke again. Finally, a taxi stopped. Just as we opened the door to get in, we heard shouting and howling from behind us. It was a group of ultra-Orthodox Jews from Kiryat Mattersdorf. They were enraged. They were shouting at us and insulting us for getting into a car during Shabbat. Some of their stones landed very close.

That night, again unable to sleep because of the time change or because of the grimy old hotel, and smoking on the narrow balcony overlooking a pitch-black and possibly abandoned Jerusalem neighborhood, I missed my sister. That Orthodox woman, with her outfit and her wig and her sermons, was not my sister. I didn't know who she was. But not my sister.

I remembered her as a girl. Her wide-eyed gaze, her turned-up little nose, her beautiful black curls. And then I remembered this: my sister, so shy in public, hiding behind my father's legs, refusing to let go of my father's legs. And then I remembered this: my sister sucking her thumb until she was ten or eleven. She sucked only the right one, and only when she was holding a worn pale yellow blanket that she—to our public delight—called her Booby, and whose lace stitching she would scratch with the fingernail of her index finger as she sucked her thumb (recently I found out, amazed, that all those years of scratching had unraveled a dozen yellow blankets). And then I remembered this: a letter that my sister had written the tooth fairy, to apprise him of our upcoming move. We're moving, she'd written. Please don't forget to come for my teeth. And then I remembered this: my sister's reaction when, after admiring him for years, she finally met Mickey Mouse in person, on our first family trip to Orlando. Look, sweetheart, here comes Mickey, my father had said. My sister looked swiftly down at the ground in an attempt to find a mouse there, and on seeing the huge creature in front of her, she burst into sorrowful tears. And then I remembered this: my sister on my mother's lap, on a private balcony at the Winter Garden Theatre on Broadway, where we'd gone one night to see *Cats*. When the show began, all the lights were dimmed and the actors, dressed as cats, made up as cats, their eyes flickering green and red and yellow like cats, slunk out and prowled stealthily through the audience. A black cat, perched on the ledge of our private balcony, was so shaken by my sister's panicked screeching that he nearly fell, and he had to come out of character and whisper to her that it was all right, that he wasn't a real cat but a regular man, a man like any other, a man who was just dressed as a cat.

Smiling, I decided to stop remembering and stubbed out my cigarette.

I was about to open the sliding glass door to the room, when yet again I heard the shrieking or wailing. So I hadn't dreamed it. There it was again, out there, down below, somewhere in that dark and abandoned Jerusalem neighborhood. It no longer sounded like a baby crying, but like many babies crying. Like a whole hospital or nursery school, I thought, where all the babies have started screaming or crying at once, almost in unison. High-pitched cries, loud, horrible, tormented. Though by turns they sounded more like the cries of an animal or a pack of animals, frightened, or dying, or about to die. I thought of the bleating of lambs. I thought of the slaughter of lambs. I thought of sacrificial lambs. Of course—I was in Jerusalem. I stood listening for a few minutes. I didn't know what to do. I couldn't figure it out. There was no light and no moon and no one around, not a single soul down on the street below. Then, maybe having given up, maybe just too scared, I turned and went back into the room. My brother slept the exquisite, motionless sleep of a little boy.

I'M DOWNSTAIRS.

It was eight o'clock in the morning. The phone had awakened me and I had to get out of bed and stumble over to the desk to answer it. It was Tamara. She told me that she was downstairs. That she knew me—laughing, teasing, alluding to the past—so she knew she'd have to come and get me. That she wanted to spend the day with me, take me to see a few sights. My brother was still in bed, in a deep sleep. I thought momentarily of the lunch and the prayer service we had scheduled with my sister and her fiancé and all of their friends and ultra-Orthodox rabbis from the yeshiva. I shuddered. Be right down, I said, and hung up.

As I got off the elevator, I saw Tamara sitting in an armchair in the lobby, her legs crossed and long and bare. I motioned to her to give me a minute and walked over to reception. She walked slowly up to meet me, and stood waiting in silence beside me as I greeted the same old man (I'd begun to view him not as receptionist but as owner, one of those cantankerous owners who don't trust anybody but themselves, or who are too stingy to pay anybody but themselves) and asked him for a yellow memo pad so I could leave a note for my parents, excusing myself. The old man looked worse than ever. His face more greenish and shriveled. His eyes red. His clothes wrinkled. His hands seemed to tremble. He was staring at Tamara beside me, still serious, still grumpy, and murmured something in Hebrew that sounded disdainful. Tamara ignored him, or perhaps she didn't hear him, or perhaps his comment wasn't that disdainful after all. She was wearing a pair of very short, old, torn khaki shorts, leather sandals, a flowing, almost see-through white linen blouse that showed the top of her freckled shoulders, and a bra that might have been red. And that was it. No makeup. Her copper hair was wild and matted, as if she'd just awakened. Her eyes were bluer than I remembered. When I finished and handed the old receptionist the note, Tamara immediately gave me a hug, an urgent hug, and this time there was no Lufthansa uniform and it wasn't awkward at all. And though part of that hug might have been retaliation for the old man's disdainful comment, I liked that she held me so tightly and so absolutely. I liked seeing her few strands of gray. I like your gray, I said, and she smiled at me with her big Mediterranean eyes. Then she took a step back and held my hands in hers, our fingers entwined, and I noted with satisfaction that she wasn't wearing a ring. But for a second, I thought I could make out a very faint circle of pale skin on her left ring finger. Perhaps I had imagined the wedding ring, in the confusion and heat of the airport. Perhaps she had taken it off that morning. Perhaps she had left it at home, hidden in some drawer or case or jewelry box. I looked up. Best not to know.

Come on, she said, tugging me outside.

Bamboo

I was drinking café de olla from a rusty blue pewter cup. Doña Tomasa had put down a matching blue pewter kettle beside me, on the sandy ground of the shack. There were no tables or chairs. The palm-frond roof was already black and full of holes. What little breeze there was stank of rotten fish. But the café de olla was strong and sweet and helped to perk me up a bit, to loosen my legs from the two-hour drive to the port of Iztapa, on the Guatemalan Pacific coast. My back felt damp, my forehead sweaty and sticky. As the heat increased, it seemed, so too did the fetidness of the air. A scrawny dog was sniffing at the ground, in search of scraps or crumbs that might have fallen onto the sand. Two bare-foot and shirtless children were trying to catch a gecko that chirped above, hidden amid the palm fronds. It was not yet eight in the morning.

Here you go, said Doña Tomasa, and she handed me a tortilla with cracklings and spicy chiltepe, wrapped

in a sheet of newspaper. She leaned on one of the sup-
ports of the shack, rubbing her plump hands on her
apron, burying and unburying her feet in the warm
volcanic sand. She had salt-and-pepper hair, a leathery
complexion, a slightly cross-eyed gaze. She asked where
I was from. I finished chewing a mouthful, my tongue
stunned by the chiltepe, and said I was Guatemalan,
just like her. She smiled politely, perhaps suspiciously,
perhaps thinking the same thing I was thinking, and
turned her eyes up toward the cloudless sky. I don't
know why I always find it hard to convince people,
to convince myself even, that I'm Guatemalan. I suppose they expect to see someone darker and squatter,
someone who looks more like them, to hear someone
whose Spanish sounds more tropical. And I never pass
up any opportunity to distance myself from the country either, literally as well as literarily. I grew up abroad.
I spend long stretches of time abroad. I write about it
and describe it from abroad. As though I were a perpet-
ual migrant. I blow smoke over my Guatemalan origins
until they become dimmer and hazier. I feel no nostalgia, no loyalty, no patriotism—despite the fact that,
as my Polish grandfather liked to say, the first song I
learned to sing, age two, was the national anthem.

I finished the tortilla and the café de olla. Doña
Tomasa, having taken my payment for breakfast, gave
me directions to a patch of land where I could leave
my car. There's a sign, she said. Ask for Don Tulio,

she added and walked off without saying good-bye,
dragging her bare feet as though they were weighing
her down and muttering something bitter, perhaps a
little tune.

I lit a cigarette and decided to walk awhile along the
Iztapa highway before returning to the car, a classic Saab,
sapphire-colored, which a friend often loaned me for
traveling around the country. I walked past a stall selling cashews and mangoes, an abandoned gas station, a
group of dark-skinned men who stopped talking and
just looked at me askance, as though resentful or perhaps
bashful. The earth wasn't earth but little bits of paper
and wrappers and dry leaves and plastic bags and a few
discarded green almonds, crushed and rotting. In the
distance, a pig wouldn't stop squealing. I kept walking,
slowly, unconcerned, noticing a mulatta woman on the
other side of the road who was too fat for her black-and-
white-striped bikini, too chubby for her high heels. All
of a sudden, I felt my foot touch something wet. Maybe
because I was looking at the mulatta, I had stepped in
a red puddle. I stopped. I looked left into a dark and
narrow warehouse and saw that the floor was covered in
sharks. Small sharks. Medium sharks. Blue sharks. Gray
sharks. Brown sharks. Even a couple of hammerhead
sharks. All of them seemed to be floating in a mire of
brine and guts and blood and more sharks. The stench
was almost unbearable. There was a girl on her knees.
Her face shone with water or perhaps sweat. She had

her hands deep inside a big gash in the white belly of a shark and was pulling out organs and entrails. In the back, another girl was rinsing down the floor with the weak stream of a hose. It was the fishermen's cooperative, according to a badly painted placard on the wall. Every morning, I presumed, the fishermen of Iztapa brought their catch there and the two girls cleaned it and cut it up and sold it. I noticed that most of the sharks no longer had fins. I remembered having read somewhere about the international black market. They called it finning. I'll have to be careful later, I thought, in the sea. It seemed to be a day for sharks.

I TOSSED THE CIGARETTE BUTT nowhere in particular and returned to the car, hurrying, almost running away from something. As I drove, I noticed that I had already started to lose the image of the sharks. It occurred to me that an image, any image, will inevitably start losing its clarity and its strength, even its coherence. I felt compelled to stop the car right there in the middle of the town and try to find a notebook and pencil and write it down, capture it, share it through words. But words are not sharks. Or maybe they are. Cicero said that if a man could go up to heaven and from there contemplate the whole universe, the wonder that such great beauty caused him would diminish if he had no one to share it with, no one to tell it to.

After a couple of kilometers on a dirt road, I finally found the sign Doña Tomasa had told me about. The land belonged to an indigenous family. The house was made of sheet metal, bricks, broken tiles, cinder blocks with exposed rusty rebar. There was a plot of maize and beans, a few palm trees looking grim and sad. There were chickens running free. A white goat was chewing the bark of a guava tree that it was tied to with a length of iron wire. Under a canopy, sprawled out on the ground, three young women were husking corn as they listened to an evangelist preaching on a small portable radio.

An old man approached, tanned and taciturn and still muscular despite his age. Don Tulio? I asked. At your service, he replied without looking at me. I explained that Doña Tomasa, the lady from the shack, had sent me. Right, he said, scratching his neck. A boy age five or six appeared and hid behind the old man's legs. Your son? I asked, and Don Tulio whispered yes, the youngest. When I held out my hand, the boy lowered his gaze and blushed at such a grown-up gesture. I opened the trunk of the car and started to take out my things, and at that moment, as though rising up from an abyss, as though muffled by something, perhaps the dryness or the humidity or the already inclement sun, I heard a series of guttural cries. I fell silent. I heard more cries. Far away, behind the house, I caught sight of an older woman, whom I took to be Don Tulio's wife or mother, helping a fat and half-naked young man as he lurched forward and fell on the floor like a drunk, kept crying out like a drunk, and headed straight toward us. He was struggling to walk toward us. He wanted something from us. The lady, using all her strength, was determined to stop him. I looked away, out of respect, or pity, or cowardice. Nobody else seemed very concerned.

Don Tulio said it was twenty quetzales, for the whole day. I took a bill out of my wallet and paid him, still hearing the young man wail. Don Tulio asked if I knew the way to the beach on foot, or if I wanted his son to accompany me. I was going to say that I didn't know, thank you, when suddenly the young man shouted something that I couldn't understand but that sounded coarse and painful, and Don Tulio immediately rushed off. The young man, now spread-eagle on the ground, was having spasms, as though epileptic. Finally, the old man and woman managed to drag him off and haul him around behind the house, out of sight.

Though they were quieter and more distant now, I could still hear the howls. I asked the boy what was happening, who the young man was, if he was ill or drunk or something worse. Kneeling down, playing with an earthworm, he ignored me. I put my things down on the ground and slowly, cautiously, headed toward the back of the house.

The young man was in a bamboo cage, lying in a puddle of mud and water or possibly urine. I could hear

all the flies buzzing around him. This one turned out
bad, whispered Don Tulio when he saw me standing
next to him, but I didn't know whether it was a moral
or a physical judgment, whether he was referring to
some perverse behavior or alcohol habit, to a nervous
condition or a mental deficiency. I didn't want to ask.
I watched the young man in silence through the thick
bamboo bars. His pants were wet and half-open. His
chin was white with saliva, his chest covered in small
fistulas and sores, his bare feet muddy and filthy, his
eyes red, tearful, almost closed. I thought that a poor
indigenous family had no choice but to keep him away
from the world, to remove him from the world, building him a bamboo cage. I thought that while I could
take a day off and drive two hours from the capital to a
beach on the Pacific for no other reason than to go for a
swim, this young man was a prisoner to something, to
some kind of evil, or alcohol, or dementia, or poverty,
or something much bigger and more profound. I wiped
the sweat from my forehead and eyes. Maybe because
of the crystalline coastal light, the cage suddenly looked
sublime to me. Its craftsmanship. Its shape and resil-
ience. I came a little closer and gripped two of the bamboo bars tightly. I wanted to feel the bamboo in my
hands, feel the warmth of the bamboo in my hands,
feel the reality of the bamboo in my hands, and perhaps
not feel my own indifference, nor the indifference of an
entire country. The young man writhed briefly in the

puddle, stirring up the swarm of flies. His moans were now docile, resigned, like those of an animal that has been mortally wounded. I let go of the two bamboo bars, turned around, and walked to the sea.

The Birds Are Back

I arrived at the Martínez house well into the afternoon, at just that moment when the sky recedes, and
the street dogs bark on their corners, and at the house
next door an evangelical preacher, aided by a broken
microphone and a loudspeaker, starts up his frenzied
shouting and chanting.

The door was opened by a short, dark, elderly woman
with a friendly face and a blue apron she'd probably
been wearing all day. You're Señor Halfon, she said.
Please come in. I'm Ernestina, Iliana's mother, she said,
holding out her hand. Iliana and her father won't be
long, she told me. They just went to check on his coffee
plants, not far at all.

Doña Ernestina closed the door behind me and we
stood there in a dark narrow hallway. To one side was
a leatherette sofa. To the other, directly across from
the sofa, the wall was covered with small family photos, now faded and matte; also on the wall were four

large high-school diplomas, all in a row, all proud in their wood and imitation gold-leaf frames. Doña Ernestina talked me through each photo, pointing as she explained—over the evangelical shouting and chanting—which of her four children was in each one, and at what age, and where they were, and what they were doing, and whose piñata it was. You see, my husband, Juan, used to love taking pictures, she said nostalgically. Before, she said, her voice suddenly a bit hoarse, and she said no more. But that last word seemed to hang there, framed among all of the photos and diplomas, like a gateway to something, perhaps to another time, another memory, another corridor, one even darker and narrower, one with no way out.

The Martínez home—humble and immaculate—was on a fairly steep hill in La Libertad, a hard-to-reach town with a temperate climate in the Guatemalan highlands, in the department of Huehuetenango, just a few kilometers from the Mexican border. A notoriously dangerous and violent part of the country: in the past few years, because of narcotrafficking; during the armed conflict of the seventies and eighties, because of military abuses and massacres; at the turn of the twentieth century, because of the revolutionary wars fought against president and despot Manuel Estrada Cabrera (years later, Miguel Angel Asturias would use him as the model dictator for his novel, *El Señor Presidente*). In 1915, the very town of La Libertad, then called Florida, was the setting for the last revolutionary battle against Estrada Cabrera's army. The revolutionaries didn't win that last battle, but they succeeded in establishing peace and freedom in the region, and in 1922, in their honor, once Estrada Cabrera was out of power—before dying, he'd been declared insane by Congress and forced to resign—the name of the town was officially changed to La Libertad.

The evangelist's sermon suddenly ratcheted up. The front door opened. Iliana walked in smiling, wiping her just-washed hands on the legs of her canvas trousers. She apologized for being late and I said that there was no need, that her mother had kept me entertained. Isn't that right, Doña Ernestina? And Doña Ernestina blushed slightly. Did you find Pensión Peñablanca? Iliana asked, and I said that I had, that I appreciated it, that I'd left the sapphire-colored Saab there along with my belongings. It's the only pensión in town, she said, but it's not bad. And besides, she said, the co-op is close by, right on one side of the main plaza, and so is Doña Tuti's café. You can have breakfast at her café, no worries. It's a safe bet. Just ask someone where Doña Tuti's is, she said. Because there's no sign.

She was a small friendly woman, Iliana, with skin even darker than her mother's. She must have been thirty or thirty-five. I'd pictured her much older. Perhaps because of the seriousness of her e-mails. Or perhaps because of the enormous responsibility and

quality of her work managing the local coffee growers' cooperative: the first co-op in the region, set up
in 1965 by a group of men—including her father, Juan
Martínez—who owned small coffee plots. I asked Iliana where her father was, and she was about to say
something, when Doña Ernestina raised her arm, as
though requesting permission to speak, and whispered: That's Osmundo. Her index finger pointed to
the photo of a young couple in a garden, he seated
in a plastic chair, she on his lap. There was a silence,
both from us and in the neighbor's evangelical cries.
As though he too had heard Doña Ernestina whisper
and was waiting for her to keep going. But Iliana was
the one to break the silence. That's Osmundo and his
fiancée, she said. Osmundo was my brother, she said.
He was murdered.

The evangelist began chanting about God and His
mercy and Doña Ernestina said dinner was almost
ready.

His name was Hitler. He was splayed out on
the kitchen floor tile, before the wood-fire stove that
was flickering and crackling and heating the comal. I
crouched down. I scratched his chin and heard him purr,
and only then did I discover a short black mustache that
looked penciled in below his little white snout.

There were five sisters. One was making tortillas

and greeted me from the comal, smiling timidly as she clapped out a tiny ball of masa. Two more were slicing lemons and avocados. Another darted in and out, chasing her three- or four-year-old daughter; she lived with her husband in the house across the way, she explained, on the other side of the street. Iliana told me to sit down, pointing to a small wooden bench painted red and pushed up against the wall. I thanked her, taking in the women's serene choreography, and thinking about my sister, and my brother, and our own choreography, and thinking that that smell—coffee, smoke, pine, coal, ground maize—was the closest thing there was to the smell of family.

Juan Martínez walked slowly into the kitchen. He was wearing an orange shirt—neon orange, fiery orange, even fierier against his toasted skin. Iliana introduced us and he held out his hand in silence. His hands were leathery campesino hands. His thin body gave the false impression of fragility. He had a sad withdrawn look, and it was a moment before I realized it was the same look Iliana had. He invited me to sit beside him on the small wooden bench.

Please excuse me, Don Juan whispered, and leaned in a bit closer to me, as though about to tell me a secret. The two of us only just fit on the bench. In front of us, the women had nearly finished cooking dinner. None of them seemed to notice the neighbor's evangelical cries. We were out checking on my coffee plants, Juan said, out on my farm. Then added: San Andrés Farm, it's called. And he smiled an enormous white smile.

Don't pay any attention to him, Eduardo, Iliana said from the stove. That's what he named his little coffee plots. She turned to us. You see, my father loves naming things, she said.

Don Juan crossed his arms and sat watching his five daughters. Iliana Lucía, he suddenly whispered. Iliana because we saw that name in the paper, and Lucía because that was the name of a nun who used to come out from the capital back in the eighties to teach the town's children. He paused for a moment. Judit Orquídea, he said, pointing with his eyes. Judit because my wife was always taken by Judit in the Bible, for her bravery, for her dedication, and Orquídea because someone told us that was the name of a flower, and what a pretty name for a girl, no? Another daughter scurried by, once again chasing after the three- or four-year-old girl, and Don Juan took her hand and held it in his as he spoke. Regina Guadalupe, he said. Regina because that was the name of the American nun who used to teach our catechism class, and Guadalupe, Señor Halfon, because my family is very devoted to the Virgin of Guadalupe. He kissed his daughter's hand, let it go, and glanced over at the comal. Patricia Amarilis, he said. Patricia just because my wife always liked that name, and Amarilis because in those days there was a woman who used to come to town, a teacher, and she was never able to have her own children, so she asked my wife to name a daughter Amarilis for her, and that's what we did, in her honor. Hitler had roused himself and was now prowling around our feet. I pulled him onto my lap and the cat got comfortable between my thighs and then dozed off almost immediately. Teresina Mancruz, said Don Juan. Teresina was a nun who came to Huehuetenango to teach the village children to read, and Mancruz, Señor Halfon, because back then we used to listen to the radio, since there was no electricity in town and radios ran on batteries, and Mancruz was the name of the protagonist on a Mexican soap opera. Don Juan smiled, and I realized that he still hadn't said anything about the name of his only son, the son in the garden photo, the dead son. But I didn't dare ask. Instead, I just asked him why he'd named his farm San Andrés, and Don Juan smacked his lips, as though to thank me for my complicity, and then whispered that it was for a priest he'd met when he was young, there in town. Father Andrés, he added. A good man, he added. I suddenly thought I saw his eyes begin to get misty, but the kitchen was dark and smoky and I couldn't be sure. We kept silent for a moment, and I got a fleeting urge to hug Don Juan Martínez. Maybe for consolation. Maybe for his nostalgic tone and his sad and subtle sense of humor. Or maybe for reasons much more my own.

ON THE DINING ROOM TABLE sat a roast chicken with pineapple and herbs, whole potatoes in butter, avocado crescents, hot tortillas wrapped in a dish towel, and a jug of coffee. In Guatemalan towns, it's customary to drink watered-down coffee with dinner.

Iliana's sisters helped set the table and then left. Doña Ernestina sat at the head of the table, said they had all had their dinner earlier, and only poured herself a cup of coffee. Hitler, on the prowl and begging under the table, was going crazy with all the food smells. The evangelist was still delivering his sermon, providentially muffled by the thick adobe walls and a light drizzle falling on the corrugated tin roof. As Doña Ernestina dished me out a little of everything, I asked Don Juan how the co-op got started and he said it had been a project of the Maryknoll Fathers, a North American Roman Catholic missionary congregation that was very committed to helping Guatemalan communities in the sixties and seventies. He said that's how they got their name, Cooperativa Esquipulas, after the famous Black Christ of Esquipulas, the town's patron saint. He said, looking at his wife, that they had both worked with the Maryknoll Fathers quite a bit. I was their driver, he said, and Ernestina their cook. That was many years ago, he said, spreading avocado on a tortilla. Before all the priests had to flee the country, he said, during the difficult years—Don Juan's euphemistic way of referring to the decades of war between the guerillas and the army. Well, said Iliana, the priests who got out in time, at least, before they were murdered or disappeared by the military. We remained silent a few seconds, as though cautious in the face of so weighty a topic. Or as though in memory of the many priests murdered and disappeared. The Maryknoll idea was that if we started a co-op, said Don Juan, that if all the small coffee growers in the region banded together, if the poor united, then we'd be stronger and more able to compete with the two or three big plantations, the rich ones. Don Juan took a sip of coffee, and I thought briefly of the word solidarity, a word that to me, until that moment, had been nothing but an old, worn-out word, a word in disuse, a word from another generation. And were they right? I asked. Did the Maryknoll idea work? Don Juan took another sip of his thin coffee, put down his cup, softly stroked Iliana's forearm as she sat on his left, and said: Now, after almost fifty years of having to endure trouble and persecution and extortion, I can say that yes, Señor Halfon, it worked.

I ATE IN SILENCE, attempting to piece together—through the narrative chaos and the neighbor's evangelical ruckus—the onslaught of trouble and persecution and extortion. Don Juan, salting a potato: The co-op almost went under during the difficult years. Doña Ernestina, snatching the shaker from her husband: At that time, holding meetings was very dangerous. Don Juan, in a sad voice, an invisible shaker still in his hand: In the difficult years, saying the word co-op was almost like saying a bad word. Iliana, sucking on a leg bone: Plus, for years there were several directors who stole money from the co-op. Doña Ernestina, refilling my coffee without asking: The last one, a man from right here, stole over a million pesos. Don Juan: Getting rid of him took a lot of doing, but we finally got rid of him. Doña Ernestina: In this country, it's hard to be honest. Iliana, with Hitler's front paws on her knees: Then came the coffee crisis, in 2001 and 2002. Don Juan, shaking his head: During those years, the New York Stock Exchange told us we had to sell a quintal of coffee for fifty dollars. Iliana, caving in, giving Hitler the bone: Today we know exactly what a quintal of our coffee costs. Don Juan, grabbing a lime wedge: Some Englishmen came. Iliana: That is, today we know that producing a quintal of our coffee costs a coffee grower one hundred and twenty-five dollars. Don Juan, squeezing the lime onto an avocado crescent: You see, some Englishmen came to conduct an economic study, and that's what they told us, one hundred and twenty-five dollars per quintal of coffee, net cost. Doña Ernestina: Imagine, the coffee growers worked for two whole years just to lose money. Don Juan, with avocado fingers: But those men from the New York Stock Exchange, who had never in their lives so much as laid eyes on a coffee plant, still made money. Iliana, smiling: That's right. Don Juan, also smiling: Nothing new, right? Doña Ernestina, standing: And that's when the Italian showed up. Don Juan, with a sigh, almost in unison: The Italian showed up. Doña Ernestina, now far from the dining room, maybe far from it all: You tell him, Juan, the story of the Italian. Hitler, as though terrified and hiding under the table, meowed.

AN ITALIAN CAME TO TOWN, Señor Halfon, a charming, handsome man, and he discovered that our coffee here is very high-quality, what they call strictly hard bean, which means intense flavor and very aromatic. He made an offer to the co-op members, to promote our coffee in Italy. We gave him a small sample and he took it to Italy, and after some studies and analyses, he confirmed that indeed, due to the type of soil and the altitude and the local climate, coffee grown here was quality coffee. Then the Italian succeeded in getting Italy to label our coffee premium-quality. A great achievement, Señor Halfon. A gold seal for our co-op. The Italian signed a contract with us and began selling our coffee throughout Italy as luxurious, special, very expensive coffee. He took it to fairs and festivals. He sold it in gourmet shops. The bags of coffee, I remember, came in a very pretty package, which said that part of the profits went to the indigenous of the Guatemalan highlands. His contract with us was for four years. During those four years, the Italian paid the co-op whatever he wanted, far below the internationally quoted price. As co-op members, we had to beg him to pay us what he had offered, what he owed us, but the Italian's payments were always low, and late. And we never saw the percentage of profits promised on those pretty packages. That's when Iliana came back. She'd been studying and working in Huehuetenango—When they murdered Osmundo, Doña Ernestina shouted, still from afar, and Don Juan, for a moment, paused, looked down, let out a long loud sigh—and we appointed her director of the co-op. As soon as she started, Iliana discovered that the co-op had just over one dollar in the bank. I'm not exaggerating, Señor Halfon. We were broke. We had an ex-director who stole. We had debts all over. We had an Italian partner who was making millions on the back of our sweat and labor. But little by little, Iliana began to impose order, and she managed to achieve several things. My daughter managed to dissolve the legal partnership we had with the Italian, though it took a lot of work. She got short-term financing for every one of the co-op members. She brought in experts from the capital to teach us how to produce better coffee, and the importance of pruning and thinning a coffee plant, and what the best varieties are, and what the best shade trees are, and why doing a soil study is vital, and how to taste the parchment beans, and how to judge a good cup of coffee. Then Iliana got funding so that every member, on their plots, could build their own wet mills, their own drying patios. She also got funds to build our office and warehouse. She forged an alliance that provided workshops for members on exporting and international commerce. But the most important thing, Señor Halfon, is that she managed to start selling our coffee abroad, our premium-quality coffee, at prices that we ourselves set. Imagine that. Now we set our own prices. This year, for example, when the international price for a quintal of coffee was one hundred and eighty dollars, Iliana managed to sell the co-op's quintales at two hundred and eighty dollars. Now, at last, we sell our coffee at the price it's truly worth. Not at the price imposed on us by New York.

DOÑA ERNESTINA RETURNED to the dining room carrying an enormous clay pot full of whole mangoes in hot syrup, and set it on the table. Four years of crops were lost, Iliana said, serving me from the pot with a large metal spoon, four years of hard work and suffering just for the Italian to make a lot of money. The syrup was exquisite. It had clove and cinnamon and a little ground allspice. But I will say, Don Juan declared as he sucked a mango pit with gusto, that thanks to the Italian, Señor Halfon, we got something very valuable. Absolutely, I said, because of him you got the international premium-quality seal, which made your co-op's coffee one of the most sought-after in the world. Don Juan wiped his lips with a paper napkin. We did, yes, but we also got something even more valuable. The evangelist preacher, in tune to some organ or accordion music, suddenly intoned: May God continue to use you for His glory. Don Juan smiled, perhaps at the evangelist's euphoric chanting, or perhaps at what he was about to tell me, or perhaps because he was a man whose smile comes naturally and means nothing. The Italian gave us faith in our product, he said. The Italian made us believe in ourselves. And if the price we paid for that was four harvests, well then, Señor Halfon, we got it cheap.

THE BLOCK ACROSS THE STREET from Pensión Peñablanca was onerously defended all night by a loud and territorial street dog. He would bark awhile, then stop barking awhile—just long enough for me to begin to doze off—then start barking again. Close to dawn, I gave up. I threw off the heavy quilt and went to rummage in my backpack for the last of my cigarettes. Smoking faceup on the bed, I watched the objects in the room gradually turn to light, come to life. I couldn't stop thinking about Don Juan Martínez, about the coffee growers, about Iliana's work at the co-op, about the pictures and diplomas hanging in the hallway, about the sisters' silent dance, about the dead brother. And once again I started thinking about my own brother, and my own sister, and our own sibling dance—an ungainly dance, an awkward dance, sometimes even a furious dance. Perhaps because of the cold, or perhaps because of the lack of sleep, all I could think of were our quarrels and fights. The early ones, flailing and hysterical, were typical of spoiled children. The later ones, with my brother, even came to blows (in the last of these, he wound up in the emergency room with a broken foot when he tried to kick me in the stomach and I blocked his kick with my elbow). The adult ones, although still violent, were now waged not with our fists but with our silence. And the most recent one, the hardest and most silent one, had been before my sister's Orthodox wedding, in Israel.

I showered and dressed slowly. When I went out, I came upon the same dog—big, black, dirty—fast asleep against the wall of a house. I considered waking him up, throwing a rock or a shoe at him. But instead I just walked up the steep cobblestone road, barely managing to sidestep several piles of lukewarm shit.

THE TOWN SLEPT ON. There were almost no pedestrians, or drivers, or buses. Shops and businesses were closed. The buildings all seemed improvised. Cinderblock facades poorly painted in primary colors. Red or grayish corrugated tin roofs. Rusted rebar sticking out of posts and columns for intended second stories. Narrow streets full of rotten fruit, paper, wrappers, plastic bags, boxes, trash from the wandering women vendors at the market the day before.

I came to the central plaza, or what had once been the central plaza and was now a paved soccer field and basketball court, the requisite lines painted on the cement, goals and baskets on either end—one sponsored by NaranJugo, the other by Frutada. I wanted to buy more cigarettes, but everything was closed. I sat down on a bench and just stared at the green of the hills and bluffs around La Libertad, a deep green, alive, the kind only seen in the rainy season. To my left was a row of shops and corner stores; to my right, the police department, painted in grays and blues, with two officers standing outside, smoking, watching me and judging me conspicuously. On the opposite side of the plaza, directly across from me, was the town church: small, gabled, its facade and bell tower painted somewhere between sky blue and bright turquoise. A woman, sitting on the steps leading up to the doors of the church, was arranging her basket to sell tostadas and atol for breakfast. Far from it all, as the backdrop of it all, a thick blanket of fog shrouded half the mountain.

SHINE. A BOY OF TEN OR TWELVE had approached me silently, from behind. Shine, he repeated, more a command than a question, and I said no, thank you. He had faint polish marks on his dark face and wore an old pair of enormous adult shoes, patent leather, and no socks. He needed both hands to bear the weight of his black wooden box of jars and dyes and waxes and brushes and dirty rags and who knows what else. Shine, mister, he said, not looking at me, almost not even trying. The two police officers were still staring at me from a distance. The woman with the basket had a stick in her pot and was stirring the atol. The boy suddenly plopped down onto the bench, at a slight distance from me, and deposited his wooden box on the ground. I asked him his name. Macario López y López, he replied decisively. Do people call you Macario? Sometimes, he mumbled. And sometimes Maca. I asked him if he knew where Doña Tuti's café was. Where're you from? the boy asked, and I said in my best Guatemalan accent that I was Guatemalan, same as he was. He smiled, not looking at me, incredulous. Don't look like it, he mumbled. Where do I look like I'm from, then? He shrugged his shoulders. Don't know, he said, not here though. I asked him if he knew the Esquipulas Co-op offices. The coffee co-op, I said. Iliana Martínez's place, I added. Do you know Iliana Martínez, Don Juan Martínez? But the boy said nothing. He stared straight ahead. Buy me a tostada, mister, for my breakfast? I noticed that the two police officers were walking toward us, by the NaranJugo goal. They were still watching me, solemn or maybe just curious. Suddenly, they flicked down their cigarettes onto the plaza, as though getting ready to do something. I slid my hand into my pants pocket and was about to pull out some change so the boy could buy a tostada from the woman, when he bluntly, almost nonchalantly, said: Oh, that Martínez family is kin of the one that got killed, right?

THE CO-OP ENTRANCE WAS a high, wide-open warehouse that served as storage unit during harvest time. From the white walls and corrugated tin ceiling hung ribbons and strings and papier-mâché streamers—perhaps a failed effort to give the place a more festive air, or perhaps they'd simply forgotten to take down the decorations after a birthday or anniversary.

I was standing in the middle of the warehouse with a coffee grower, a co-op member from the village of Chanjón, in the municipality of Todos Santos Cuchumatán, who that morning had made the long, arduous, four-hour drive to La Libertad.

Good coffee, yes? he said suddenly in an obstructed Spanish, a protracted Spanish, a Spanish molded by his Mayan tongue, Mam. We were each holding our cup of coffee. It is, I said. Very good. We appreciate it now, he said, we know how to drink it now, but before, at home, all we drank was instant coffee, or sometimes backwash coffee, pulp coffee they call it here, or sometimes we drank nutcoffee. I hadn't heard him properly or else I didn't understand. What's that? He stood silent a moment, looking up, his mouth half-open, as though allowing each of his words the time to make the leap from one language to another. That's what we called the very cheap beans brought in from the lowlands, he said, from the coast, where people from town went to work in the cane fields or in the cotton fields. He smiled weakly. He was holding an imaginary cheap bean between his thumb and index finger. We toasted them on the comal, he said, and then we crushed them with a grindstone. Tasted a little like coffee. But it wasn't coffee. That's how it got its name. Not coffee. Or notcoffee. Or nutcoffee. Something like that. That's what we used to drink, before.

Cruz Pérez Pablo was his name, and it took me a moment to realize that Cruz was his first name, Pérez his second name, and Pablo his last name. As though his entire name had been assigned backward. As though he lived back to front. Cruz Pérez Pablo. A gallant name, one that deserves to be projected onto a huge white screen. He was dressed in the traditional clothes of Todos Santos Cuchumatán: red trousers with gray stripes; a blue-and-white-striped long-sleeve button-down shirt with thick, colorfully embroidered trim down the front and on the collar; a small straw hat with a band made of the same fabric. I stood looking at his clothes, so beautiful, so colorful, such a proud and unequivocal symbol of his identity, although its origins dated back to Spanish rule, centuries ago, when the multiple patterns and colors were nothing but a system imposed by Spanish caciques to differentiate their indigenous slaves by territory.

He personally had prepared the two cups of coffee as we waited for Iliana and her father. Hot robust coffee, slightly acidic, slightly chocolaty. We were drinking—taking communion, I thought at the time, with coffee from his own land, coffee cultivated by his old hands—and a few members were coming and going, and Cruz Pérez Pablo would introduce them to me and they would remove their hats or baseball caps and shake my hand firmly and introduce themselves again, welcoming me to town and to the co-op, enunciating their names with pride, casting them like fruit or like a poem onto that enormous white screen.

THE BIRDS ARE BACK. The squirrels are back. The kinkajous are back. The raccoons and the coati and what people here call tusas. Really big moles. Really delicious too, if you can manage to trap them.

Don Juan Martínez was squatting beside one of his plants. As he spoke, his hands seemed to work autonomously: gathering dry leaves from the ground, pulling out grass and weeds and sickly twigs. Iliana, beside me, simply let him speak.

We'd stopped seeing birds, Señor Halfon. We'd stopped seeing animals. This hillside was all bare, completely stripped, not a tree left. You see, people had to chop down all the trees on their land in order to plant maize. Plus, he said, they needed the wood from those trees for their comales, to heat their homes, to cook. Don Juan stood. He pushed back his worn straw hat. Just look at this hill now, he said. It's full of cypress and pine again, full of shade trees for the coffee, like cushín, which is that one there, and the one over there, which is what they call inga. He lowered his arm, taking his time, and went on. Now that the co-op is up and running, coffee brings us enough money to buy our maize, so we don't have to plant it. Now our own coffee plants and our shade trees, when we prune them, give us enough wood for the comal, so we don't need to cut down any other trees. Now we plant trees, said Don Juan. And there's nothing better, Señor Halfon, than giving life. Giving life not just to coffee plants and trees, but to the mountain itself.

The three of us kept walking, single file, down a dry narrow trail lined with very green coffee plants decked with very red fruit. Iliana was pointing out which plants were arabica and which were bourbon and which were caturra. Those are the best varieties, she said. That's all I have here, on San Andrés Farm, said Don Juan, and smiled. We try to get members not to plant cataui or catimor anymore, Eduardo, since those varieties don't produce such good coffee. Don Juan stopped, crouched before a plant, and pulled off a short branch at the bottom. You have to pull out the offshoots, explained Iliana, watching her father, to thin the plant so that it produces better beans, better coffee. At first, she said, it was very difficult to make the older members understand that. Don Juan seemed to stroke the plant's trunk with affection after pulling out its offshoot. People around here were used to a plant producing a lot of coffee, said Iliana, and of course, when you remove the offshoots, that plant produces fewer beans, but those beans are much higher-quality. The plant invests all of its energy, you could say, into producing less fruit, but that fruit comes out better. As I listened to Iliana speak, as I observed her and her father, a forbidden question suddenly popped into my head, an almost biblical question, a question that must never be asked, a question that could only occur to someone with no offspring. And I swallowed bitterly. It's like pledging quality over quantity, you see? Iliana went on, and that pledge marks a change not only in the way members grow coffee, but also in the way they conceive of themselves.

Don Juan stood and we continued walking in silence among the coffee plants, traversing the slippery, uneven terrain. We heard the distant cry of a falcon, then the sweet metallic trill of a motmot, then the joyous cackling of a flock of parakeets.

We came upon some dilapidated, rotting wood huts. What's this, Don Juan? I asked, but Don Juan made no reply. Perhaps he didn't hear me. He stood before a lone coffee plant, tall and dense and bursting with red fruit. All of that, said Iliana, jerking her jaw toward the row of huts, was my brother's chicken coop. No one has kept it up for the past three years. Ever since he was murdered.

Don Juan turned his back to us and seemed to step into the enormous, lone coffee plant. As though hiding among its green leaves, searching for something among its green leaves. As though wishing the old plant would protect him. His back still to us, he was plucking beans off the old plant, slowly, tenderly, his campesino hands letting the red fruit fall soundlessly onto the dry ground. He bent a little and picked the lower beans. He stretched to the upper branches, pulled them toward him, and his expert hands stripped them clean. The ground around his feet was turning red. His straw hat crackled in the branches. He now looked more hunched, smaller. He kept on plucking beans and dropping them onto the ground. He kept entering the foliage of the old plant, the greenery of the leaves and branches, until the whole of him disappeared entirely.

White Sand, Black Stone

The young officer was reading the pages of my passport diligently, scrupulously, as though they were the pages of a gossip magazine or a cheap novel. He held them up. He looked at them against the light. He scratched them hard with the nail of his index finger. It occurred to me that he might fold over the corner of one of the pages at any moment, bookmarking it, as though planning to return to his reading later. You travel a lot, he said suddenly, as he looked over all the stamps. I didn't know whether this was a question or an observation and so I remained silent, watching him sitting there in front of me, on the other side of a black metal desk. He couldn't have been twenty. His face was beardless, dark brown, gleaming. His green khaki uniform fit him too tightly. He seemed unbothered by the beads of sweat that ran slowly down his forehead and neck. So you like traveling, he mused without looking at me, in the contemptuous tone of a new soldier. I considered telling him that all our journeys are really one single journey, with multiple stops and layovers. That every journey, any journey, is not linear, and is not circular, and it never ends. That every journey is meaningless. But I didn't say anything. Through the open door I could make out the noise of motorcycles, trucks, vans, a ranchera being sung on a transistor radio, thunder in the distance, swarms of flies and mosquitoes and men shouting offers to buy and sell Belizean dollars. Revolving in the corner, an old floor fan simply circulated the humid afternoon jungle heat.

It was my first time there, in Melchor de Mencos, the last Guatemalan town before crossing into Belize. I had left the capital early in the morning, and driven to the border stopping only once, at the halfway point, at Lake Izabal, to put in some gasoline and have some lunch—a seafood broth, a handful of dark tortillas with queso fresco and loroco flowers, and plenty of coffee.

Señor, your place of residence? the officer asked me all of a sudden, still looking through the pages of my passport and jotting down my details in a huge accounting ledger. Guatemala City, I lied, although it wasn't altogether a lie. And the reason for your trip to Belize? I'm going to visit some friends, in Belmopán, I lied, although that wasn't altogether a lie either: I had been invited to give a reading at the University of Belize, in Belmopán; traveling by land had been my idea, to get to see the road, to get to know Belize's beautiful

white-sand beaches, Belize's idyllic turquoise blue sea—
an idea that now, having seen the distance and the terrible state of the highways, I was starting to question.
And your profession, señor? Engineer, I lied, as I always
lie, as I always write on immigration forms. It's much
more advisable and prudent, especially at a border of
any kind, to be an engineer than a writer.

The officer said nothing, and slowly, with all the
lethargy of the tropics, he continued to note down my
details.

Outside, it was cloudy and thick and the sky looked
ready to burst. After wiping my forehead with my
hand, I started looking at a huge map of Guatemala
that was stuck on the wall just behind the officer, and
I remembered how, as a boy, in the seventies, I had
won a prize at school for having drawn the best map
of the country. My drawing, of course, still included
the then province of Belize, the largest one, located in
the far north. It wasn't until 1981 that Belize gained
its independence—and until 1992 that it was recognized by Guatemala—thereby ceasing to be the upper
part of the map that I'd learned to draw as a boy. I
was never very good at drawing. But that one time,
I remember, I really made an effort. And my prize,
which I took with some astonishment from the hand
of my teacher, was a small green mango. I still can't
see a map of the country without thinking of a green
mango. I still can't see a map of the country without

thinking that Guatemala, in a more than figurative sense, had been decapitated.

No good, señor.

It took me a moment to understand that the officer, without looking up and barely audible over the wheezing of the fan, was talking to me.

What did you say? I asked. I said this is no good, he said, closing my passport and dropping it onto the metal desk as if in disgust, as if it were something stiff and rotten. Your passport, señor, it expired last month. I felt a light blow to my gut. That's not possible, I stammered. The officer, impassive, just kept scribbling something in the old ledger. Was it possible? How long had it been since I'd gotten it? How long since I'd even checked the expiration date? I reached out and picked up the blue booklet from the desk and opened it to the page. It had indeed expired a month ago. No good, the officer muttered down toward the ruled yellowish pages of the old ledger, and for a moment I thought he meant that what wasn't any good was me. So what now? I asked. So what now what, señor? he replied without looking at me. Is there no other way I can get into Belize? None, señor. I can't cross the border with my ID card? He shook his head just once, definite. Belize, he said, is not a part of the Central America agreement. It was true. All the Central American countries had recently signed an accord allowing their citizens free passage across their borders—all of them, of course, except Belize. I sighed, already picturing the drive back to the capital, already calculating all the hours and all the kilometers here and back, crossing almost the entire territory of Guatemala here and back, all in a single day. I opened my leather pouch to put the passport away and was surprised to see the red cover there. It hadn't occurred to me. In fact, even if it had occurred to me, I usually leave that red one at home, and I wouldn't have expected to find it there, in the leather pouch I always travel with, and in which I keep other credit cards (just in case), my medical insurance card (just in case), my diving license (just in case), a couple of condoms (just in case). I gave a triumphant smile. Here you go, I said to the officer, and I held it under his gaze, over the same pages of the ledger. What's this? he spluttered, confused, still suspicious. I am many, I said to him somewhat satirically. But today, I said, I am two.

The officer, perhaps for the first time, raised his eyes, and looked at me slowly, skeptically, as I held a booklet in each hand, a passport in each hand: the Guatemalan one in my right, the Spanish one in my left.

Excuse me, he said, and stood up. On his green khaki back the dark round patch of sweat was growing.

He walked slowly toward a bigger and more important desk, at which sat a bald gentleman, plump, with a thick ash-colored mustache and reading glasses, dressed in the same green khaki uniform. His boss, I presumed. The young officer handed him the passports and pointed at me and the two men began to go through my documents, comparing them, judging them, whispering I don't know what. Suddenly, the older officer took off his reading glasses. He looked up and stared at me for a few moments. As though something in me had enraged him. Or alarmed him. Or as though trying to find something in my face, perhaps some detail or expression that would prove my identity. Then he lowered his gaze, handed my passports back to the young officer, and feeling for the reading glasses hanging around his neck, returned his attention to the papers on the desk.

Sign here, said the young officer no sooner than he had sat down, pointing at an empty line on the ledger, beside my name. I signed with relish, in a flowery, stylized hand. The officer stamped the ledger way too hard, maybe with the rage of the defeated, and handed me both passports. Next, he shouted toward the line of people who were waiting their turn behind me. I put everything inside the leather pouch, turned away unhurriedly and, without saying a word, as I was leaving the immigration office, already hearing the drops of rain on the corrugated tin plates of the roof, I noticed that the mustached officer was watching me gravely over the top of his glasses.

Outside, it was raining hard. I quickly dodged the sellers of chewing gum and other sweets, the sellers of

sour oranges sprinkled with pumpkin seed, the sellers of Belizean dollars with wads of dirty bills in their
hands and little nylon pouches tied around their waists,
and I started running through the pelting rain to where
I had left the old sapphire-colored Saab. As soon as I
arrived, I opened the door and got inside and hurriedly
stuck the key in and started the engine. I sat still, half-
soaked in rain, or perhaps half-soaked in sweat, just listening to the sudden shower hit the bodywork, and to
the thunder in the distance of the Petén jungle, and to
the unbearable metallic clicking of a dead battery.

YOU'RE GOING TO HAVE TROUBLE finding a trucker
who'll help you here.

His accent sounded Salvadoran, or perhaps Nica-
raguan. He was wearing crocodile-skin cowboy boots.
His button-down shirt was open, and over his heart,
in green ink, he had a tattoo of another heart with an
arrow through it, encircled by a ribbon with somebody's name. His woman, I presumed. Or one of his
women. He had a long machete in a black leather
sheath hanging from his belt. And immediately, as I
saw him approach and smile at me with his silver teeth,
I felt a flash of distrust and panic and I was about to
close my eyes and say please, just the money, let me
keep my credit cards and the rest of my papers. But he
quickly greeted me and told me that his truck was that

one over there, the white one, that he was headed for Mexico, that his name was Roldán. I didn't want to ask if that was his first or last name. Nor did I want to ask what he was carrying in his truck.

I'd had to sit in the car for nearly an hour, waiting for the rain to subside. From time to time, I would open the door a little to air out the heat and my cigarette smoke (the electric windows, of course, were not working). But it was raining too hard and the water would rush in at once and so I had to fester in there for an hour, submerged in my own smoke and steam. On several occasions, I thought I saw—through the windshield and the sheets of rain—the mustached officer standing at the door of the immigration office, maybe watching the rain shower, maybe watching me.

No trucker here is going to give you a hand, said Roldán. My compañeros will say they're in a hurry. He scratched his stomach. But they're making it up, he said. They're just a bit cruel.

With a couple of whistles, he summoned over a teenaged kid who was walking past. You, help me push, he told the teenager, who reluctantly agreed. You put it in neutral, Roldán shouted to me, and when I say, shift to second and try to start it up. We tried three times. The engine didn't even respond.

Oh boy, said Roldán, widening his silver smile. That battery won't go anymore, mi rey. The kid, without a word, had made himself scarce.

I got out of the car. I held the pack of Camels out to Roldán and he took a cigarette and we both stood there a moment, smoking in silence. The sun had come back out. In the distance, a veil of warm mist covered part of the mountain. Have you got jumper cables? he asked me suddenly. I think so, I said, in the trunk. My truck has a twenty-four-volt battery, he said. We've got to find a driver with a twelve-volt battery. Maybe we'll be able to charge it up. He asked for another cigarette. For later, he said, and put it behind his ear. So where are you coming from? he asked, and I explained that I'd left the capital that same morning, that I was on my way to Belize, that I wanted to cross over to Belize, that I wanted to get to the white-sand beaches of Belize. Not with that battery, mi rey, he said, still smiling. But don't you worry. We'll figure it out right away. God willing.

Roldán stopped two truckers, and from their cabs both of them merely shook their heads and went on up the highway. Soon the owner of the truck that was parked next to me arrived. Roldán approached him and explained the situation and the guy said that yes, he had a twelve-volt battery but that he couldn't give me a jump. Why not, old man? Roldán asked, and the guy just shook his head, reluctant. But Roldán was so insistent that the driver finally agreed. We connected the two batteries. The trucker started his engine, and we let it run for a few minutes. Nothing. Then we left it running a few minutes more, and I tried again, and again, nothing. The trucker detached the cables and got up into his cab and, almost offended by me, as though I'd stolen something from him, went on his way.

Roldán took out his cell phone and dialed a number. He asked for a tow truck. Don't worry, he told me. It's a friend, he said, who can quickly change your battery here in Melchor de Mencos, on the other side of the bridge, and you can continue on your way to Belize.

I felt something in my knees. Maybe impotence. Maybe a devastating solitude. Maybe the panic of being drawn, further and further, into a grand spiderweb of swindlers.

Roldán stood smoking beside me until his friend arrived with the tow truck and then he negotiated a price with him and warned him to treat me well. I thanked him. I offered him a few bills, which he stubbornly refused. I said, perhaps out of fear at finding myself alone and stranded in the middle of the Petén jungle, that he should let me buy him a beer in town. I've got to be going too, he said, shaking his head.

I climbed into the passenger seat of the tow truck. It smelled of sweat, of grease, of rancid fish, of burned-out brakes. From the rearview mirror hung a pink plastic crucifix, a laminated postcard of a blonde with her tits out, and two furry dice, one white and the other black. I read the writing on the windshield, along the top in big gold letters: CHRIST IS MY NORTH. Don't even think about going on to Belize tonight, Roldán said, holding my door. Better to stay in town, have a tasty dinner, get a good night's sleep, and leave nice and early tomorrow morning, in no rush. I felt that same something in my knees again. We'll see, I said. I closed the door. Seriously, he shouted over the tow truck's hefty engine. It can be dangerous, out at night.

IT DIDN'T LOOK LIKE a mechanic's workshop. There was no sign anywhere. The place was nothing more than a small lot with an earthen floor, enclosed by three adobe walls and a big gray metal gate that opened out onto the road. There were tools lying around and piled up all over. Parked in one corner was a Mercedes-Benz from the seventies, possibly white, all rickety and rusty. Next to it, a little boy age two or three was sitting on the floor, completely naked. He was playing with a handful of pegs and nuts. The guy with the tow truck was also the owner and the only mechanic there. He was named Nicasio. After hooking the battery up to an old machine, he confirmed that it was indeed unusable now. He told me he could get ahold of a new one, a luxury one, imported, at a very good price. That I should pay him half up front and leave the keys to the car with him. That I should give him a few hours, that there was a diner on the corner where I could wait, have something to drink, and he'd come and get me when he'd finished the work. I looked at my watch. It was already five in the afternoon. Then I looked at the car: open, weary, its innards exposed. I took my backpack out of the trunk and headed for the gate. The naked boy watched me, sprawled out in a puddle of mud.

I WALKED TO A LITTLE PARK at a fork in the road. There was no one there. There was no breeze, no shade, no respite. At the entrance, badly painted on a dirty white archway, a sign welcomed me to the town. I took my last cigarette out of the pack and sat down to smoke on a bench that was still a bit wet. Almost immediately, a young man approached carrying bags full of nuts and an old set of bronze scales. Anything for you, señor? I've got peanuts, he said. I've got fava beans, cashews, macadamias, salted almonds. I bought a couple ounces of cashews. After weighing them and taking my money, he sat down beside me. I asked him about the origin of the town's name, Melchor de Mencos. They say that it was the name of a general who defeated the British, he said, centuries back. But who knows if that's true, he said. He looked up at the highway, as though searching for someone, or as though someone were searching for him. I also looked out toward the highway. I saw a man with dark brown skin, taking small steps forward, as though dancing forward. Then I saw a truck carrying a scraggy white cow on its flatbed. Then I saw three kids on a single bicycle. And you're just passing through?

the young man asked me. Something like that, I said. I finished my cigarette in silence.

I walked past a girl who was slobbering red and chasing after a group of chicks. Her white dress looked like it was already stained red. Her loose white stockings also looked like they were already stained red. Her headband and her black patent-leather shoes lay forgotten behind her by the open door of an evangelical church, through which came the chanting of the parishioners and the preacher. The girl was holding half a pomegranate in her dark hands. Suddenly, she brought the half pomegranate to her mouth and took a big bite and started to fire little red pellets at the chicks.

I walked past a man leaning up against the trunk of an almond tree. He was sitting on the grass, his legs stretched out. He was, I assumed, taking advantage of the tree's shade. He was wearing black pants and a white shirt with a black tie. He had a newspaper on his lap. As I came closer, I saw that he had a green circle on each temple. They were two slices of lime, held there with a shoelace tied around his head. Little drops trickled all down his face, perhaps of lime juice or sweat or both. Come here gringo and let me suck it, I thought I heard him whisper behind me as I hurried away from the almond tree. But when I looked back, the man seemed to be fast asleep.

I WENT INTO A LITTLE STORE on the town's bustling main road. An elderly man was leaning on the counter, barely upright, barely holding an almost empty bottle of Quetzalteca Especial aguardiente. Can I help you? said a squat lady from the other side of the grille. I walked over. I greeted her, seeing through the grille that she sold only domestic cigarettes. I asked for a pack of Rubios. The elderly man muttered something. The lady passed the pack to me through the grille, and then I passed her a few bills. The elderly man came toward me a bit and muttered something again, holding out his hand. He smelled of urine. Don't bother the gentleman, the lady scolded him. And you just ignore him, she said to me, handing me back a few coins through the grille, which I immediately wanted to give the elderly man. But his old hand couldn't hold them and the coins fell to the floor. I crouched down to retrieve them. When I stood back up, right there beside me was the mustached officer from immigration: still serious, still in his green khaki uniform, still with his reading glasses hanging around his neck, but now in the company of a man in cowboy boots and a cowboy hat and with huge shades and a toothpick between his teeth and a black pistol well tucked into his waistband. I wiped my forehead with the sleeve of my shirt. I took off, almost at a run, into the gloom of the main road.

AN ENORMOUS RED MACAW was perched on a broomstick at the back of the diner. From time to time, it scratched at its chest with its beak or let out a cry or a sharp screech. Its red feathers looked dull and sad. On each of the four tables, on a floral plastic tablecloth, was a bottle with an atomizer. In case, the girl said as she seated me. It's just that the bird's a little crazy, she said, looking at the enormous macaw. Sometimes it just attacks people, she explained. But a spray of water will scare it off.

I opened the new pack of Rubios and lit one and immediately started to feel better, to breathe easily again. From the kitchen, behind a bead curtain, I could hear the murmuring of women's voices, laughing, groaning, a merengue on the radio, the clinking of plates and glasses. A couple of white lightbulbs hung from the ceiling. The macaw looked sleepily at me from its perch.

The same girl came out through the bead curtain carrying a tray. She walked over to me. I noticed that she was barefoot. I noticed that she now had a baby tied to her back (or did she before and I hadn't seen it?) with a long blue sash. The baby was sleeping. Here you are, she said, and placed on the table an ashtray, a bottle of

Gallo beer, a small glass. I thanked her. You're welcome, she said. You don't want to eat anything? she asked me, almost embarrassed, and I said not now, but thanks, maybe later. A stray dog tried to come into the diner, but she scared it away with a clap. Then she just stood where she was, holding the tray flat against her ample breasts, perhaps waiting for something. I asked her why it was called the Fallabón Diner. That's what they call this neighborhood, she said. Years ago, she told me, Fallabón used to be its own village, right here, but now it's a part of Melchor de Mencos. (I learned later that the name of the village, Fallabón, comes from a fire and explosion that had taken place near there, in a timber warehouse, in 1950; it's an Anglicism, from the English words fire and boom.) The baby whined and the girl reached back and stroked its cheek with a finger. So is that your car, in Don Nica's workshop? It is, I said, reluctant to explain to her that it wasn't really my car, but a friend's. She clicked her tongue, as if to say good luck, or as if to say what a shame. I asked her if she could recommend a hotel, since maybe I'd have to spend the night, and she thought a moment and then told me that La Cabaña Hotel was good, that it was close by, on the main road. There's even a pool, she said. La Cabaña Hotel, I repeated, so as not to forget, and wiping the sweat from my forehead with a paper napkin, I thought I saw something small and dark climbing the back wall. Perhaps a spider. Perhaps a horsefly.

Perhaps a scorpion. And is that yours, the macaw? I asked the girl. She smiled. It's just part of this place, she said, but I didn't understand whether that meant the restaurant or the neighborhood or the whole town. Does it have a name? Sure, she said. Gómez, she said. The macaw screamed something, maybe because it had heard its name and wanted to join in the conversation. I stubbed my cigarette out in the ashtray. So he's male? I asked the girl and she just gave a laugh and shrugged and said probably, nobody really knows. I saw that the floor tiles under the macaw were covered in gray-and-white droppings. Excuse me, whispered the girl, and went back into the kitchen.

I poured myself a swig of beer with plenty of foam. The beer was warm but it went down well. I poured myself another swig. I lit a cigarette and took a deep breath. I moved the bottle of water closer, just in case the macaw decided to flap down off the broomstick. I opened my backpack and was about to take out a book to read for a bit, when I felt the presence of somebody standing behind me.

You, kid, bring us two beers, yelled the immigration officer.

THEY EACH ACKNOWLEDGED ME STERNLY, with just a glance, and positioned themselves at a table in front of me. The girl came out through the bead curtain.

She carried a bottle of beer in each hand. The baby was still sleeping, tied to her back. Here you are, Don Francisco, she said. The officer muttered something, perhaps thanking her. He had taken a red handkerchief out of the pocket of his green khaki uniform. He finished wiping the sweat from his neck and his face. Then he took a long sip of beer and wiped his lips and his grayish mustache with the red handkerchief. The other man reached out and grabbed the girl's forearm hard and pulled her over toward him until she was sitting on his lap. Do you have pork carnitas? he asked her in a lecherous whisper, his long-nailed hand holding her neck, like a hook. His voice sounded too feminine to me. We do, she said, never looking up from the floor. The baby on her back stirred, whined. And do you have cracklings? Them too, she said, her voice muted, her gaze still fixed on the floor. Well then, go bring us one portion of carnitas and another of cracklings, he said, and gave her a shove toward the kitchen. She tottered a little. Right away, she said, recovering her balance. The man took off his shades and his cowboy hat and took out the black pistol and put them all down on the table. Still chewing on the toothpick, he raised his right hand as though swearing an oath before a judge. And if that fucking bird comes anywhere near me, he said, I swear to God I'll put a couple of bullets in him.

Both men laughed loudly, almost cackling, perhaps

looking at me. The girl slipped away quickly, head down, the baby swaying on her back.

I wanted to smoke. I noticed the cigarette I was holding in my fingers was shaking slightly. I couldn't stop looking at that dirty hand in the air, and as I looked at it, I suddenly thought of the heart attack my Polish grandfather had suffered at the end of the seventies. I was very young at the time, but I can still remember my mother's uncontrollable weeping when she got the call from the hospital. My grandfather had been lucky. It was only a minor attack. He recovered quickly. And as a result, following the three instructions he received from his doctor, he quit smoking, started drinking a couple of ounces of whiskey daily (for his nerves, he used to say), and got into the habit of walking. He walked a lot, every morning, for exercise. He would leave the house very early and walk around his neighborhood. Sometimes for up to two hours. Sometimes I'd go with him. And during one of those walks, while he was alone at the end of the Avenue of the Americas, right by the statue of Pope John Paul II, a motorcycle with two guys on it stopped beside him. They knocked him to the ground, he told us later, outraged. They gave him a blow to the head, he said, showing us where. They wanted to kidnap him, he said, perhaps now exaggerating what had been a simple robbery. They took everything he had on him, he said, now indignant, or almost everything, now proud. He managed to keep the ring with the black stone that he wore on his right pinkie finger. Sometimes he told us he had pleaded with them till they let him keep his ring. Sometimes he told us he had struggled with them to keep his ring. Sometimes he told us he had fought with them to keep his ring. Which version he told depended on the passing of the years, or on his nostalgia, or on his mood, or on the character of the person who was asking him (my grandfather understood, maybe at an intuitive level, that a story grows, changes its skin, does acrobatics on the tightrope of time; he understood that a story is really many stories). He had bought that ring in 1945, he liked to tell us, in New York, the first stop on his journey to Guatemala after being freed from Sachsenhausen concentration camp. In New York, at a Jewish jeweler's in Harlem, he had paid forty dollars for it. And he had worn it for the rest of his life, for the next sixty years, on his right pinkie finger, as a way of mourning for his parents and siblings and friends and all the others exterminated by the Nazis in the ghettos and concentration camps. A few years back, when my grandfather died, that ring was left to one of my mother's brothers, who wept when he inherited it and decided to keep it in the safe in his office. It was just an old black stone in an old gold setting. But one night, someone broke into that office and managed to open the safe and stole everything inside, including my grandfather's ring with the black stone.

And there before me, on the pinkie finger of that dirty hand now holding a tortilla filled with pork and cracklings, was a ring very much like my grandfather's ring. Or perhaps it was exactly the same as my grandfather's ring. Perhaps it was exactly the same black stone, and exactly the same setting in gold metal, and it was exactly the same shape and size. Or at least it was all exactly like the ring in my memory, the ring as I recalled it or as I wanted to recall it, on my grandfather's pale and slightly crooked right pinkie finger. And although I knew it was impossible, even preposterous, even absurd, I couldn't help imagining that this ring, on this greasy hand, was indeed my grandfather's ring with the black stone. Not a similar one. Not an exact replica. But the same one. The one my grandfather had bought in New York, in Harlem, in 1945. The one he had worn for the rest of his life on his right pinkie finger. The one he had managed to save after convincing or compelling—at the end of the Avenue of the Americas, at the end of the seventies—some muggers or maybe kidnappers. The one that, when he died, was inherited by one of my mother's brothers. The one that had been stolen from a safe one night by a thief who never knew what he was stealing; by a thief who never knew that in that insignificant and somber black stone, one could still see the perfect reflections of my grandfather's exterminated parents (Samuel and Masha), and the faces of my grandfather's exterminated sisters (Ula and Rushka), and the face of my grandfather's exterminated brother (Zalman), and the faces of so many exterminated men and women and boys and girls and babies who were killed as they slept in the arms of their mothers, as they dreamed in the gas chambers; by a thief who never knew that in that small black stone it was still possible to hear the murmur of all these voices, of so many voices, intoning in chorus the prayer for the dead.

The macaw shrieked and stretched out its wings and, still on its perch, started to flap them energetically, desperately, as if wanting to fly.

White Smoke

When I first met her at a Scottish bar, after who knows how many beers and almost a whole pack of unfiltered Camels, Tamara told me that she liked to have her nipples bitten, and hard.

It wasn't actually a Scottish bar, but an ordinary bar in Antigua, Guatemala, that served only beer and was called (or at least known as) the Scottish bar. I was sitting at the counter, drinking a Moza. I prefer dark beer. It makes me think of dark taverns and sword fights. I lit a cigarette and she, on a stool to my right, asked me in English if she could have one. I guessed by her accent that she was Israeli. Bevakasha, I said, which means you're welcome in Hebrew, and I held out a box of matches. Immediately, she became friendly. She said something in Hebrew that I didn't understand and I made it clear that I could say only a few words and recite a prayer or two and count to ten. Fifteen, if I tried. I live in the capital, I said in Spanish to show her that I wasn't

American, and she confessed, perplexed, that she'd never thought there was such a thing as Guatemalan Jews. I'm not Jewish anymore, I said smiling, I retired. What do you mean, not Jewish anymore, that's not possible, she shouted in that way Israelis often shout. She turned to face me. She was wearing a white Indian-style blouse made of light cotton, well-worn jeans, and yellow espadrilles. She had copper-colored hair and emerald blue eyes, if there's such a thing as emerald blue. She told me that she'd recently finished her military service, that she was traveling through Central America with her friend, and that they'd decided to stop in Antigua for a few weeks to take some Spanish classes and earn a little money. Her, she pointed. Yael, her friend, a very pale and very serious girl with beautiful shoulders, was the one who'd served my beer. I said hello and they started speaking in Hebrew, giggling, and at some point I thought I heard them mention the number seven, though I didn't know why. A German couple walked in and her friend went over to serve them. She held my hand tight, said that she was pleased to meet me, that her name was Tamara, and then took another one of my cigarettes without asking.

I ordered another beer and Yael brought us two Mozas and a plate of potato chips. She stood in front of us. I asked Tamara what her last name was. I remember it was Russian. Halfon is Lebanese, I said, but my mother's maiden name, Tenenbaum, is from Poland,

from Łódź, and they both shrieked. It turned out that
Yael's last name was also Tenenbaum, and as they were
verifying the information on my driver's license, I
considered the remote possibility that we came from
the same family, and envisioned an entire novel about
two Polish siblings who believed their family had been
exterminated and then, after not seeing each other for
sixty years, were suddenly reunited thanks to two of
their grandchildren, one a Guatemalan writer and one
an Israeli hippie, who met accidentally at a Scottish bar
that wasn't really a Scottish bar, in Antigua, Guatemala.

Yael took out a liter of cheap beer and filled three
glasses. They handed me back my license and we
toasted—to us, to them, to the Poles. We fell silent,
listening to an old Bob Marley song and contemplating
the never-ending brevity of the planet.

Tamara lifted my lit cigarette from the ashtray, took
a long drag, and asked me what I did for a living. I told
her with a straight face that I was a pediatrician and a
professional liar. She held up a hand, as if to say stop.
I really liked her hand and I don't know why I recalled
the verse of an e.e. cummings poem that Woody Allen
quotes in one of his movies about infidelity. Nobody,
I said, trapping her hand like a pale, fragile butterfly,
not even the rain, has such small hands. Tamara smiled,
told me that her parents were doctors, that she sometimes wrote poems too, and I guessed she had attrib-
uted the cummings line to me, but I didn't feel like
setting her straight. And she didn't let go of my hand.

Yael filled our glasses and I smoked awkwardly with my left hand as they spoke in Hebrew. What's wrong? I asked Tamara, and with a disconsolate pout she told me that someone had stolen her stuff the day before. She sighed. I spent all morning walking around the craft market, she said, through some ruins, all over the place, and when I sat down on a bench in the Central Park (that's what people in Antigua call it, even though it's really a plaza), I realized that someone had slashed my bag open with a knife. She explained that she'd lost a little money and some papers. Yael said something in Hebrew and they both laughed. What? I asked, curious, but they kept laughing and speaking in Hebrew. I squeezed her hand and Tamara remembered I was there and told me that the money didn't matter as much as the papers. I asked what papers. She smiled enigmatically, like a Dutch girl selling tulips. Four hits of acid, she whispered in bad Spanish. I took a sip of beer. Do you like acid? she asked, and I said I didn't know, that I'd never tried it. Tamara spoke euphorically for ten or twenty minutes about how essential acid was as a way to open our minds and turn us into more tolerant, peaceful people, and all I could think about while she blathered on was of tearing her clothes off right there in front of Yael and the Germans and any other Scottish voyeur who might care to watch. To get her to stop talking, and to calm myself down, I suppose, I lit a cigarette and passed it to her. The first time I tried acid, with my friends in Tel Aviv, she said as we passed the cigarette back and forth, I got really drowsy, very, very relaxed, and I think I saw God. I seem to recall she used the Spanish word Dios, although she might have used Hashem or God or Adonai or YHVH, the unpronounceable all-consonant tetragrammaton. I didn't know if I should laugh, so instead all I did was ask her what it looked like, the face of God. He didn't have a face, she told me. So what did you see? I asked. She said it was hard to explain and then closed her eyes and took on a mystic air and awaited some divine revelation. I don't believe in God, I said, wakening her from her trance, though I do speak to Him every day, or just about. She turned serious. You don't consider yourself a Jew and you don't believe in God? she asked reproachfully, and I just shrugged and asked what for and went to the bathroom before there was any chance to start on such a pointless topic.

As I STOOD OVER THE TOILET, I saw that despite being slightly drunk I had a limp erection. There was a dark puddle at my feet. An old lightbulb hung from the ceiling. The wall in front of me, behind the only toilet, was full of colorful graffiti—words and sayings and names and drawings and even poems. My eyes immediately searched for anything crossed out, anything forbidden, and I recalled the canvasses of Jean-Michel Basquiat, who wrote words on them and then crossed some out, so you'd see them more, he said—the very fact that they were obscured, he said, made you want to read them. I washed my hands, thinking about my grandfather, about Auschwitz, about the five green numbers tattooed on his forearm that throughout my entire childhood I'd believed were there, as he himself had told me, so that he wouldn't forget his phone number—his way of crossing them out, I suppose, of forbidding them. And I thought about Łódź, about his apartment in Łódź on the first floor of a building on the corner of Zeromskiego Street and Persego Maja Street, number 16, near the Zielony Rynek market, near Poniatowskiego Park, in which he and his girlfriend Mina and their friends were playing a game of dominoes when the German or Polish soldiers captured them all one afternoon in November of 1939. And I thought about the way my grandfather's face looked both cynical and disappointed every time I told him that I wanted to visit Poland, Łódź, the Zielony Rynek market, his apartment on the corner of Zeromskiego Street and Persego Maja Street, where that afternoon he saw his siblings and his parents for the last time, and where, in November of 1939, after that game of dominoes was interrupted, he'd never returned. What do you want to go to Poland for? he used to say. You shouldn't go to Poland. The Polish betrayed us.

Familijny Mleczny Bar. That's what I saw in another city, outside another bar, painted in gold letters on the glass of the front door. Milk bar, I remembered having read someplace before traveling to Warsaw. Classic Polish cafeterias. Very communal. Very cheap. Vestiges of another time, a time more austere and less globalized. I was standing on Nowy Swiat Street—which means New World in Polish, I later learned—freezing in pink in the premature night, watching diners through the enormous front window: them too mostly vestiges from another time. The last bastion, I thought. The last refuge of the old world, I thought, right here in the middle of this strange new world. Everything inside was glowing in the night. Everything looked warm, and comfortable, and delicious. I could see that the menu, written on one wall, was only in Polish. Suddenly, a young couple walked in. I acted on impulse and walked in with them.

The line moved quickly—first to the window where a redheaded woman, void of any expression whatsoever, was taking orders and payment; and then to a second window, which opened directly onto the kitchen, and through which customers took their plates. I tried to read the enormous menu written on the wall, but I couldn't decipher or even recognize the name of anything. We kept moving. In front of me, the two young people were taking off their gloves and scarves and caps and preparing to order. I turned to the tables and noted that everyone was eating quickly, in silence, with near-mechanical movements and expressions. Maybe they were enjoying their dinner, but they seemed determined not to let it show. Briefly, out of the corner of my eye, I saw a pink ghost in the glass, and it took me a moment to realize that I was that ghost, still wearing the pink coat. The young couple finally reached the first window. They ordered their meals and paid the woman. Now it was my turn. I didn't know what to do, or what to order, or what to say. I leaned over to the couple and asked them if they spoke English. A bit, said the man, and I felt less nervous. I asked him if he could order for me. He stood staring at my huge pink coat, perhaps thrown by my huge pink coat, and I sensed the increasing anxiety of the old people behind me waiting their turn and found myself on the verge of shouting to the man that I was hungry, that my damn suitcase had gotten lost. But luckily all I said was that I didn't speak Polish. He consulted with his partner. They both had shaved heads, were dressed in black, had tattoos on their arms and necks and rings in their lower lips. What do you want? I told him that it didn't matter, that he should decide, that I'd have the typical. Soup? Yes, of course, soup. And maybe a kielbasa? Yes, that too, a kielbasa. And black tea? Yes, thank you, black tea, and I listened to him order it all from the redhead at the first window. I also ordered you some dessert, he said. You'll like it, he added. Naleśniki z serem, that's what it's called, and he smiled. I thanked him again and they moved up a few steps toward the second window. The redheaded woman said something to me that I didn't understand but took to be the grand total of what I owed her for my dinner. I gave her a few bills, a few złotys, and she, still tight-lipped, and still wearing no expression whatsoever, and as stiff and automatic as her old cash register, handed me my change.

I sat down between two old Poles, without taking off my pink coat. I thought they both looked a bit like my grandfather. I tried not to see them as traitors, not to judge them, not to condemn all old Poles. I made a futile attempt to forget my grandfather's words. And warming up as I ate dish after dish (the best one: that dessert, which turned out to be a Polish version of crepes or blintzes), I finally realized that my entire dinner had cost a little less than two dollars. The great mathematics of socialism.

BOB DYLAN'S VOICE WHINED in the background. Tamara was singing. Yael had filled my glass again and was now flirting with a guy who looked Scottish and who quite likely was the owner of the bar. I kept looking at Yael. She had a silver belly-button ring. I pictured her in military uniform, toting a huge machine gun. I turned and looked back, and Tamara was smiling at me as she sang. Her, I could only picture naked.

I took a long swallow and emptied my glass. An old indigenous man had walked into the bar and was trying to sell machetes and huipiles. I told Tamara that I was running late but that we could meet the following day. Can you come back here from the capital? she asked. Sure, I'd love to, it's only thirty minutes by car (I'd parked the Saab out on the street). All right, she said, I get out of class at six. Should we meet here? Ken, I said, which means yes in Hebrew, and I gave her a half smile. I love your mouth, it's shaped like a heart, she said, and then she stroked my lips with her finger. I said thank you, and told her that I really liked my lips stroked with a finger. I do too, Tamara whispered in her bad Spanish, and then, still in Spanish and baring all her teeth like a hungry lioness, she added: But what I like even more is having my nipples bitten, and hard. I wasn't sure if she really understood what she was saying or if she'd said it as a joke. She leaned into me and made me shiver with a kiss on my neck. I wondered what her nipples looked like, if they were round or pointy, pink or vermilion or maybe translucent violet, and standing up to leave, I said in Spanish that it was a shame, because when I bite them, I bite them soft.

I paid for all the beers and we agreed to meet right there, at six o'clock. I gave her a tight hug, feeling something that has no name but is as loud and clear as the white smoke from the Vatican on a dark winter night, and knowing full well that I wouldn't be back the next day.

Surviving Sundays

It was raining in Harlem. I was standing on the corner of 162nd and Amsterdam, my coat already damp, my old umbrella barely holding out against the sudden gusts of wind. It was almost four in the afternoon, and already starting to get dark. I didn't know Harlem. I didn't know which way to walk. I didn't know which direction would take me to Edgecombe Avenue, in Washington Heights. I just stood there looking up the street as if I might be able to recognize something in the rain and the wind and the premature December dusk. I hunched under the umbrella. With some difficulty, I managed to light a limp, rain-specked cigarette.

Heading to Marjorie's, I presume.

Her presence beside me, all stoic, gave me a start. She seemed not to mind the rain. Or not to know it was raining.

You're heading to Marjorie's, I presume, she said again, taking a pair of thin black woolen gloves out

114

of her bag. But you don't know how to get there, she added, and took a long black woolen scarf out of her bag. I could tell by looking at you.

Her English sounded faintly accented. Caribbean, perhaps. African, perhaps. The skin on her face was deep black and flawless and probably still silky smooth. The whites of her eyes shone in the gloom. Only the slight gray in her hair—a short Afro—gave away her age.

Is it that obvious? I asked, and she did up the buttons on her black raincoat and folded her arms and said she could tell by the day, by the time, by the subway station on the corner of 162nd and Amsterdam, by the expression on my face, by the fact that there was always one to be found standing there, on that corner. She took out of her bag a black felt cloche hat, bell-shaped, 1920s style. You always find someone looking lost in the middle of Harlem? I asked her. Or you always find someone with an expression on his face that says he's desperately searching for the way to Marjorie's? And I smiled with a mixture of shame and solace. Something like that, she said. Come on. It's this way, child. She had already started to walk. I hurried and took a final drag on my cigarette and, crushing it out on the ground, discovered with pleasant surprise that under the thick folds of her black raincoat, splashing indifferently through the puddles, was a pair of bloodred cowboy boots.

SO IT'S YOUR FIRST TIME, THEN?

I was surprised at how slowly and gracefully she walked. As if following a rhythm. As if she were a model on a catwalk: elegant, exotic, aware of being watched. As if she were in no hurry to arrive and get out of the rain. Several times I offered her my umbrella—flimsy and fragile in the wind—but she didn't notice, or didn't care, or didn't want to get too close to a stranger. Rain was dripping from the brim of her cloche hat. I was still entranced by her bloodred boots. Perhaps because of the bloodred color. Perhaps because I'd never myself owned cowboy boots. Too spineless.

Yes, my first time, I said. A friend sent me a postcard, I told her, with a photo of Marjorie in a long turquoise dress, or maybe a mint green dress, I said, and ebony hands, and the address of the apartment on Edgecombe Avenue, I said, but without telling me much more. I considered getting out the postcard and showing it to her, as evidence. You don't know who Marjorie is, then? she asked. I said sort of, said that I knew a bit. We stopped on the corner of 161st and Amsterdam. Look, they're heading over there, she said, pointing at a couple holding a folded map. And them too, pointing at another group of pedestrians. And him, she said, pointing at an older gentleman in jacket and tie and carrying a big black case. How do you know? I asked. She smiled or almost smiled in the darkness. Many a Sunday, child.

The light changed and we began to cross the street.

Marjorie Eliot, that's her name, she said. For years she's been opening her apartment on Sundays, every Sunday, without taking a break or a vacation, ever since one Sunday back in 1992, when her son died. She fell silent. A sharp gust of wind struck us head-on. Every Sunday a jazz concert, she continued. Parlor jazz. At four in the afternoon. In the living room of her own apartment. With different musicians. The musicians come and go. Novice musicians and famous musicians and musician friends of hers. And it's always free. She always welcomes anyone who wants to come to her home and listen to a couple of hours of jazz, and that's a lot of people. She paused, took a deep breath, and with a soothing, almost secretive voice, she whispered: And all that to honor the memory of her son, through music.

We turned left. She asked me my name. Very pleased to meet you, Eduardo, she said. My name's Shasta. There are some names that shimmer, it occurred to me then, or perhaps it occurs to me now. There are names you long to shout. She asked me where I was from and I told her Guatemala, that I was only in New York for a few days, just passing through. I considered telling her I was there, passing through, to receive some Guggenheim money—God love it, wrote Vonnegut, or Vonnegut's narrator—that soon, if I ever got over my fears and demons, I would use to travel to Poland, to Łódź, my grandfather's hometown. But I didn't say any more. And she didn't ask any more, accustomed, I'm sure, like all New Yorkers, to the fact that everybody there is just passing through, that everybody there is on their own ridiculous pilgrimage, that the whole world is nothing but a handful of salt.

We crossed St. Nicholas Avenue. That way, she said, signaling with a glance, is St. Nick's Pub, Harlem's legendary jazz club. Ah, the old Poospatuck, I said, and she, looking askance, almost complicit, threw me a half smile. I knew something about the history of St. Nick's Pub. I knew that when it first opened, in the thirties, it was called the Poospatuck Club, after a tribe native to New York. Later, in the forties, it was named the Rendezvous, by its new owner, Charles Luckeyth Roberts, or Luckey Roberts, the great stride pianist, whose span on the keys was so wide and so quick, it's been said, because he had the skin between his fingers surgically cut. Later, in the fifties, adding opera to the repertoire, the new owners called it the Pink Angel—because, it's been said, it was a popular haunt for homosexual men. And lastly, since the sixties, St. Nick's Pub.

We came to Edgecombe Avenue. On the far side of the road was a small strip of trees. On the far side of the trees was a highway. From the far side of the highway, in the distance, we could perhaps hear the gentle flow of the Harlem River. We turned right. I didn't say anything, hoping she would talk more, simultaneously eager to arrive and wanting never to arrive. Almost at once, she stopped at the black door of a huge classical building, and gave me a look. A look filled with something. Kindness, perhaps. Weariness, perhaps. The skin on her face, because of the humidity or because of the light coming from an ancient streetlight, seemed to burn in the night. She said: Marjorie Eliot says she started to host jazz concerts in her apartment, after the death of her son, as a way of surviving Sundays.

NUMBER 555 EDGECOMBE AVENUE has many names. Some call it the Paul Robeson Residence. Others, the Roger Morris Building. Others, the Triple Nickel. Still others, Count Basie Place. Built in 1916, for its first twenty-five years it was a segregated residence: whites only. But around 1939, when Harlem's character changed, so did the rules and restrictions at 555 Edgecombe Avenue, and it became the residence of distinguished and famous members of Harlem's African-American community. Like musician Count Basie. Composer and pianist Duke Ellington. Sax player Coleman Hawkins. Writer Langston Hughes. Judge (and the first African-American on the Supreme Court) Thurgood Marshall. Baseball player (and the first African-American in the major leagues) Jackie Robinson. Boxer (and the first African-American on the pro golf circuit) Joe Louis. Singer Lena Horne. Writer Zora

Neale Hurston. Actor and political activist Paul Robeson. Pianist Marjorie Eliot.

Go on in, child, go on in.

She had taken out a bunch of keys, had opened the heavy black iron door.

I closed my umbrella and went quickly inside as she held the door for a group of tourists, then guided them toward the elevator, told them to go on up to the third floor. I stood looking at the lobby: large, ostentatious, the whole place clad in green, gray, and beige marble, with friezes sculpted in plaster and meticulously adorned in gold leaf. On the walls were poorly maintained gaudy bas-reliefs of chubby children at play, and chubby children with flutes, and chubby children riding on the backs of goats. There was a huge stained-glass window in the ceiling, also in poor condition. When I was a little girl, she said to me, looking upward and shaking the water from her raincoat, they decided to paint black over it and cover it with wood planks. She took off her gloves. She took off her cloche hat. She ran a hand through her short salt-and-pepper Afro, while the pink tip of her tongue emerged and ran over her top lip, then her bottom lip, maybe licking away the raindrops. To protect the window, she said. From an expected atomic bomb.

We walked over to the elevator. And as we waited for it, I imagined her as a little girl, growing up there, playing and running in the lobby and in the corridors and surrounded by all the gilded children and all the famous residents of the building and always wearing her bloodred boots.

Have you known Marjorie a long time? I asked. Yes, a long time, she said. She was a good friend of my parents. I considered asking who her parents were, whether they still lived there. But I thought it inappropriate. On Sundays, I help her out however I can, she said. Sometimes I set out the chairs. Sometimes I put in the blue lights. Sometimes, during the break, I serve the orange juice and cookies to the guests. Sometimes, I help a few lost souls find their way. She gave me a graceful smile. It's my way, however small and useless, she said, of honoring the memory of a dead son. She fell silent, and it occurred to me that she'd said these last words with a different voice. Perhaps with a voice that was trembling, or hoarser, or breaking slightly. Perhaps with the restrained and false voice of a ventriloquist. And I knew then, with absolute certainty, with total conviction, that she too had lost a son.

The elevator doors opened, we stepped inside, she pressed the button, and we went up slowly, in silence. Both of us looking straight ahead, both of us looking up, both of us looking again at her bloodred boots, and feeling or imagining that we were feeling, in this space that was no space, in this small antechamber, the devastating and heroic strength of a mother for her dead son.

Suddenly, a bell rang. The doors opened. Here's where you get out, she said, I go on to the top floor. I was a little surprised. I'd assumed that she was also going to Marjorie's, that she'd be accompanying me to Marjorie's, and I told her so. She shook her head. Not today, she said. Today, I survive alone.

I stepped out into the hallway. In the distance I could hear, sounding muted, muffled, the sweet and dissonant melody of a piano. I turned to the elevator, to Shasta. I thanked her. On the right, she said, apartment 3F, and hurry, child, you're already late. The sound of the piano stopped, then silence, and gentle applause. She smiled at me with just her eyes. I held out my hand, a bit hurried and proud, perhaps wishing to defer the inevitable for a while longer. It took her a moment to understand, but then she also held out hers. And we stayed like that for a couple of seconds, maybe not even that, each of us on separate sides of the doors.

Prologue at Saint-Nazaire

I'm looking out at the submarine base. In 1940, here, in Saint-Nazaire, a port town on the French Breton coast, the German Kriegsmarine erected this enormous base for building submarines. The famous U-boats, as they are called in English, or U-Boote, in German, an abbreviation of Unterseeboote. I look down through the window and I can see, directly opposite, the gray-brown block, oblong, dismal, vast (three hundred meters long, eighteen meters tall); then I turn my gaze to the pieces of paper scattered over my desk, photocopies of the correspondence between Chekhov and his friend Pleshcheev.

It is January 1888. In a letter to poet Alexei Pleshcheev, Anton Chekhov remarks on the process of writing "The Steppe," his first long story. He tells him that writing long things is extremely tedious and much more difficult than writing trivial things. He also tells him that, in order to earn a little money, he is considering writing something short for one of the newspapers, perhaps for the *Novoye Vremya*, perhaps for the *Peterburgskaya Gazeta*. His friend Pleshcheev writes back at once, dismayed. He tries to dissuade him. He insists that it would be a great shame to put his long story aside and write something trivial just for the money, for newspapers that are read one day, he writes, and used as wrapping paper the next.

I watch a group of children running around on the roof of the submarine base. An outing from some French school, I think, and I think about the word trivial, about the importance of the trivial in art, in literature. Isn't the trivial, after all, the raw material of the short story writer? Aren't anecdotes that seem trivial— that is to say, insignificant—the very clay with which the short story writer carries out his craft and shapes his art? All of life, I think, is codified in these trivial, minuscule, transparent details—details that seem not to contain anything of importance (a leaf of grass, wrote Walt Whitman, is no less than the journey-work of the stars). A great short story writer, I think as the children play on the old submarine base, knows how to make something immense of the brief, something transcendent of the insignificant, knows how to transform nothing at all into a few pages that contain everything. I recall now a story about Chopin that Ingmar Bergman told when somebody asked him why he made intimate movies, movies about couples, why he made chamber cinema instead of bigger, more epic productions. At the end of a concert, said Bergman, a lady asked Chopin a similar question—why he didn't write operas or symphonies instead of his short preludes and nocturnes. And Chopin replied: Well, madame, mine is a small kingdom, but there I am king.

I turn my gaze back to the papers on my desk.

It's January 1888. Chekhov receives that letter from his friend Pleshcheev, arguing against triviality, insisting that he continue with his long, serious story. And Chekhov writes back to him: Many thanks for your kind, sweet note. What a shame it didn't come three hours earlier. Just imagine, I was scribbling a poor tale for the *Peterburgskaya Gazeta*. As the first of the month is approaching, with debts to be paid, I played the coward and sat down to write a piece of work in haste. But it doesn't matter: the story took me no more than half a day.

This rather poor tale, this triviality that was a mere six folios in length, this piece of work written in haste that only took half a day's work and seemingly no effort at all, ended up being one of his masterpieces, the story "Sleepy".

I look at the pieces of paper in disarray on my desk, some of them already crumpled, some of them stained with coffee rings. I see the Chekhov book, open to the first page of that story. Night. That simple, that dry. With a single word, he begins this story about dreams and delirium, violence and poverty, crying out for life and crying out for death; about the nameless boy and the nursemaid Varka, who lulls him in his cradle; about children.

I look outside again, down from this tenth-floor window. There are seagulls in the air. At the Loire docks, I watch the coming and going of yachts, sailboats, tugboats, small fishing vessels, cargo ships. There's a drawbridge, which at the sound of a bell is raised and opens the way to the locks. There is a grand-looking white cruise ship (*Norwegian Epic*, it says in sky blue letters), anchored down, surrounded by cranes, in the final stages of construction. I think about another cruise ship (the *Champlain*), which, setting out from this same port, transported another Russian writer, in 1939, to New York (Nabokov recalled with nostalgia the gardens of this Breton town). But the only thing that interests me is the old submarine base. I look at it, and it's easy to imagine the black submarines coming in and out beneath the Loire's waters. Multiple swastikas fluttering in the sea breeze. And my Polish grandfather, still a young man, still skinny after his release from Sachsenhausen concentration camp, close to Berlin (there's a black-and-white photograph of my grandfather in Berlin, soon after his release from Sachsenhausen: young, thin, dressed in jacket and tie, riding a bicycle on some deserted Berlin street; he isn't smiling, but the expression on his face is serene), getting ready to weigh anchor from here, from Saint-Nazaire, to America: first to New York, where he spent a few weeks, where he bought the black-stone ring he would wear for the rest of his life, on the pinkie finger of his right hand, as a sign of mourning; and then, just because he had an uncle there, to Guatemala. And it's also easy to imagine my Polish grandfather walking over and around that imposing gray-brown cement structure—a structure, in fact, that proved indestructible. It could never be knocked down. Not by the constant bombardments of the Allied aircraft (which did manage to flatten most of the town of Saint-Nazaire). Nor later by the French themselves, who continue to insist that its demolition would have been extremely costly, almost impossible, due to the roof and walls of reinforced concrete, which in some places are up to nine meters thick.

The longer you look at one object, wrote Flannery O'Connor, the more of the world you see in it. And so I keep looking at the submarine base outside my window. I can't help it. Or I don't want to help it. I know there's something important in that old submarine base, something symbolic or perhaps poetic, something at once ephemeral and indestructible. Like in a story. Like in a good story. I see there's nobody there anymore, no children playing on the roof, no children anywhere, no longer any life.

Monastery

The clunky brown Citroën was parked in front of Hotel Kadima.

I opened the door and had to move a small suitcase from the passenger seat before I could get in. I asked Tamara what the suitcase was for. A surprise, she said, tossing it into the back. So, where are you taking me? I asked, but Tamara just started the engine and smiled again and asked about my brother. So that was your brother with you at the airport? I said that it was, that it was my younger brother, that I was fourteen months older. You look exactly alike, she exclaimed. Yes, I said, at first glance, though we're actually very different. Different how? she asked, jamming on the brakes. My brother's taller, I said. Darker. Sweeter. Freer. And he's got the hands of a god. Tamara gave a quick laugh. What about your sister? Oh, my sister, I started to say, and then stopped, thinking or maybe feeling for the perfect word. My sister is the most intrepid, I could have said. My sister is the most ethereal, I could have said, but ethereal as in mercury, as in a dry leaf in the breeze, as in those little habits like cracking your knuckles or running your tongue across your upper lip, habits that don't mean anything and at the same time mean everything. When's the wedding? Tamara asked. Tomorrow afternoon, I said, but I'm not going. She turned to me, confused. What are you saying? She was driving atrociously, erratically, speeding up and then braking violently at the last minute, jerking the gear-shift back and forth as though in a rage. I thought I might get queasy. I decided not to go to the wedding, I said, gripping the door handle tightly and overstating my resolve. I can't go, or I don't want to go, I said, I'm not sure which. She mumbled something. Maybe a reproach. Maybe just a groan. Maybe she didn't believe me. After a pause, I asked her about her friend Yael. What friend Yael? Your friend, I said, Yael, the one who was traveling with you when we first met. I don't know who you're talking about, Eduardo. When I met you, I had just finished my military service and I was traveling through Central America. Alone.

I didn't understand. I thought she was kidding. I thought about saying Yael, that girl who worked in the Scottish bar in Antigua, with my same last name, with the beautiful shoulders and the silver belly-button ring.

Tamara leaned over to the glove compartment and took out a small green box. She had no idea she'd just run a stop sign. She pulled halfway over to the curb and parked appallingly. She leaned over to the glove compartment again and took out a stack of papers or maybe postcards. Look at this. And she turned on the hazard lights.

They were black-and-white photos printed on cardboard. They still had a chemical smell. They were all out of focus, out of frame. In one I could make out the profile of a nose; in another, a half smile; in another, part of a neck; in another, one thick dark eyebrow. I didn't understand. What is this? I asked. A friend of my father took them, Tamara said. An old Jew, she said, and then, like a quick jab, she added: A blind man. She wasn't smiling. Her hands were playing with the small green box. A blind photographer? I asked. Can there even be blind photographers? A car behind us honked, perhaps insulting us for her terrible parking. His pictures are all of Palestinian children, Tamara said. He travels to Palestinian cities and towns and takes pictures of Palestinian children. Once, I went with him and my father to Ramallah. He would sit on a bench or sometimes he'd sit on the ground and wait for a boy or girl to come up to him, and then suddenly he'd hand them his camera, an old Leica. The children were as fascinated by his camera as they were by his trust and by his blindness. And while they were touching the camera,

he would reach out a hand and start touching them.
Their hair, their arms, their shoulders, especially their
faces. Slowly. Gently. With something akin to affection. He was getting to know them with his hands, I
suppose, with his touch. The children hardly noticed,
or just giggled. Then they'd give him back the camera
and he'd take a single photo of each child. Or I guess
of a single feature of each child. Very quickly. Almost
without their realizing it. Later, on our way back home,
I asked him how he decided which feature to photograph. Tamara paused, waiting for a noisy truck to pass.
First he told me he didn't know. Then, after considering it for a little while, he said that it was always the
most beautiful feature, of course. Then, after another
little while, smiling, he said one's eyes could always find
the most beautiful feature. Tamara opened her door.
Those are copies of the pictures we took that day in
Ramallah, she said. Do you like them? I was going to
say yes and no. I was going to say that Paul Wittgen-
stein, after losing his right arm in World War I (What
kind of philosophy must it take to overcome that? his
brother Ludwig wrote), not only learned to play the
piano with one hand but commissioned great compos-
ers—like Prokofiev, Strauss, Ravel—to write him oeu-
vres and concertos for the left hand. I was going to say
that, according to the notebooks of Thelonius Monk
(or Melodius Thunk, as his wife used to call him), a
genius is the one most like himself. But I just stuck the

pictures back into the glove compartment with the slew of maps and papers and candy wrappers and chocolate wrappers and something that looked like two condoms, still sealed in plastic.

Here, she said handing me the small green box. I'll be right back.

Noblesse, in white letters. Virginia Blend, in black letters.

I lit a cigarette. It was hot inside the Citroën. Perhaps because the images of those children were still in my head, I noticed two girls on the other side of the street, playing among the pedestrians. They must have been ten or twelve. Sisters, maybe, or best friends. Suddenly, one of them flung herself to the ground, head-first, and did a handstand. And just like that, straight up on her hands, nimble, she began to walk among the pedestrians. Like it was nothing. An upside-down pedestrian. A feet-up pedestrian. An inverted pedestrian. Then, still on her hands, she turned and walked back to where the other girl was. Now it was the other girl's turn. She didn't have the nerve. Her friend or sister seemed to be encouraging her, explaining to her how to do it. To no avail. The first girl stretched tall once more, raised her slender arms up into the air, and again hurled herself down, again walked feet-up among the pedestrians. Perfect. Elegant. With the precise and studied grace of a gymnast. Her legs straight. Her feet pointed way up in the air, amid all the pedestrians' heads. When she finished, the other girl clapped. They both clapped. I rolled down the Citroën's window, and as I tossed my cigarette out, it occurred to me that pirouettes are always incomprehensible. Then something strange occurred to me: that I must not forget that scene; that I must make an effort to recall the scene of the girl walking upside down on a sidewalk in Jerusalem, feet-up in Jerusalem, feet-up among the Israelis; that I must find the most beautiful feature and take a mental photograph, a blind man's photograph; that some day I'd understand why. I closed my eyes as though imitating the old photographer, as though that were enough, as though my eyelids were the shutter and just by closing them the image would be fixed. When I opened them, the two girls were racing off, zigzagging, almost leaping through the crowd, holding hands.

I LIT ANOTHER CIGARETTE. I looked at my watch. I wiped the sweat from my forehead with the sleeve of my T-shirt. The ticking of the hazard lights was starting to annoy me.

There was a homeless man on the sidewalk beside me. Old, bearded, filthy. Swathed in rags and blankets that looked like the colors of the Israeli flag. He was muttering to himself, kneeling on a piece of cardboard.

I smoked awhile before realizing that the lump beside him—small, white, stock-still—was a cat. It seemed illogical to me that a cat could be so still with that many pedestrians around. Too stiff, I thought. Maybe it was a stuffed animal. Or maybe it was sleeping. Or dead. Was it dead? I opened the door and got out.

The homeless man, two or three steps away from me, mumbled something. I approached slowly without closing the car door. I stared at the cat, willing it to move, to yawn, to stretch the way cats stretch, to do something, anything, to show me that it wasn't dead. But the more I contemplated it, lying there, inert, squalid, the more convinced I became that, in fact, it was dead. I stubbed my cigarette out on the sidewalk. I crouched down to see it better. The cat's eyes were open. It seemed not to blink. Suddenly the homeless man yelled at me, perhaps in Hebrew, most likely begging. Then he began to laugh. Loud. Then louder. His laugh was solid and abrupt, like a series of waves crashing into the rocks. He was jeering at something behind me, farther back. I turned. Not two minutes had passed, but the brown Citroën was surrounded by a group of soldiers, maybe four or five soldiers, all young, all holding guns. They were nervous. They were looking inside the car. I walked toward them and they became even more nervous and began shouting at me in Hebrew and pointing their guns at me and instinctively I put my hands up, and suddenly I couldn't hear. I couldn't hear anything. A few pedestrians began to stop, to shout at me, but I just saw mouths moving and shouting without hearing what they were shouting. I saw the homeless man still laughing without hearing his laugh. I saw one of the soldiers, a blond girl, asking me something without hearing her question. I saw Tamara approaching from a distance, running in slow motion, a plastic bag in her hands, and I felt as if someone were removing cotton balls from my ears, and slowly I began to recognize Tamara's voice, calming the soldiers in Hebrew. Saying something like this, I imagined: that she was very sorry, that the brown Citroën belonged to her, that the idiot standing there with his hands in the air was her Guatemalan friend, that he didn't know that in Israel you can't just leave an empty car in the middle of the street. I could hear the pedestrians murmuring again. I could hear the homeless man laughing again. The soldiers weren't lowering their guns. Tamara told me in English to get in the car. Right now. I got in and sat down and closed the door. She handed me the plastic bag and immediately started the engine. I apologized, distressed, but she didn't say a word. Just shook her head as we started to drive away. I wiped the sweat from my forehead, from the back of my neck. The white cat was still splayed in the same position.

IT HAS MANY NAMES, she told me as she drove, dropping pebbles of hash and strands of tobacco into a rolling paper on her leg. The Israelis call it security fence, or separation wall, or antiterrorist fence. She then licked the paper and rolled it long and tight. She was steering with her elbows. She hadn't shifted out of fourth gear for some time. The Palestinians call it the wall of racial segregation, or the new wall of shame, or the apartheid wall. And she lit the joint, inhaled. The international media, according to their political slant, call it wall or fence or barrier, depends, she said, and exhaled a sweet bluish cloud. She passed me the joint. I don't like hash. But I couldn't say no. I took a couple of drags and handed it back to her, and we fell silent, simply staring at the immense wall or fence or barrier. I hadn't pictured it so tall, so long, so thick, so imposing. It looked like it went on forever. I felt a profound desire to touch it. I was about to ask Tamara to stop, when suddenly I felt queasy. Maybe it was her driving. Maybe it was the combination of hash and the heat inside the Citroën and the adrenaline rush I'd gotten with the soldiers. Maybe it was something much darker and more fleeting. I rolled the window all the way down, stuck my head out and, breathing in the warm fresh air, thought of other walls. Chinese walls and German walls and American walls. Holy walls of temples and damp mossy walls of cells. The brick walls of a ghetto, the walls surrounding an entire people imprisoned in a ghetto, starving in a ghetto, dying slowly and silently. All of a sudden, I saw or imagined I saw on the wall (we were driving very fast and my eyes were almost closed and my pupils were dilated) the all-black figure of the girl in the Banksy painting: her black braid, black bangs, little black skirt, black shoes, black face looking up, her whole body facing up toward the sky as she floats up the wall with the help of a bunch of black balloons held in her tiny black hand. It occurred to me, my head halfway out the window and already experiencing a delicious lethargy from the hash, that a wall is the physical manifestation of man's hatred of the other. A palpable, concrete manifestation that attempts to separate us from the other, isolate us from the other, eliminate the other from our sight and from our world. But it's also a clearly useless manifestation: no matter how tall and thick the construction, no matter how long and imposing the structure, a wall is never insurmountable. A wall is never bigger than the spirit of those it confines. Because the other is still there. The other doesn't disappear, never disappears. The other's other is me. Me, and my spirit, and my imagination, and my black balloons.

Tamara gently roused me with an elbow. She offered me the joint and I took it with no hesitation, almost with relief. Regardless of its name, she said, accelerating sharply into a curve, it is what it is.

THEN EVERYTHING WAS SAND. The undulating landscape. The olive trees. The date palms. The Bedouins and camels on the side of the road. The sky and the clouds and maybe even the wind. As though we were making our way through a watercolor in which everything had been painted with the same sandy brush, on the same sandy canvas, in the same sandy color, but in endless tones and hues. Including us.

Take off your clothes.

Tamara stood in front of me. She raised her arms, peeled off her white linen blouse, and cast it to one side. She kicked once, kicked again, and her leather sandals landed on top of the blouse. She pulled down her khaki shorts, slowly, and tossed those too on top of the blouse. Take off your clothes, she commanded again, her whole body smiling in a red bikini, the freckles on her face sparkling in the sun. I began to sweat. I stuck my hands into my pants pocket. The modern bikini was invented by a French engineer, I stammered, my voice tight and idiotic, or at least to me it sounded tight and idiotic in that vast desert. By Louis Réard. In 1946. Tamara frowned. My hand unexpectedly touched a slip of paper. Réard took the name from Bikini Atoll, I blathered, the slip of paper clenched in my right fist, my right fist clenched in my pants pocket. An atoll in the middle of the Pacific Ocean, I said, where that same year the Americans carried out nuclear testing. Did you know that? I clenched the paper tighter, contemplating the shape of her legs and hips, the smooth curve of her belly, the hint of her nipples—round or pointy? pink or vermilion or translucent violet?—through the fabric of her red bikini top. Be quiet now, Eduardo, and take off your clothes. Her smile was emphatic, categorical. I assumed a slight stutter (as a friend suggested I do, during moments of crisis) and started to babble some excuse about my bathing suit, and what a shame that I didn't have it with me. Look in the suitcase, she said, turning her freckled back to me, in the backseat, she added, her feet already in the water, and you'll find two towels and a bathing suit for you. I didn't want to ask whose bathing suit it was. I didn't want to know. Best not to know. I stood still for a few seconds, the paper held tightly in my hand, watching her step like a goddess into the indigo blue sea.

WE WERE FLOATING ALL ALONE. There was nobody else there. The water was hot and oily and smelled strongly of sulfur. I was suddenly jolted by an unbearable stinging on the tip of my penis. I thought of the hash. Tamara, watching my face, as though awaiting my reaction, laughed. It burns down there, right? she asked splashing around and laughing some more. It's the salt, she said. Something the guidebooks don't tell you. It'll pass. We were floating close to each other without actually touching. She told me that although she loved the Dead

Sea, she detested the hordes of tourists. Years ago, with
some girlfriends, she'd stumbled upon this tiny private
beach. She tried to come regularly, because the salt was
very good for your skin, the salt was very good for many
things. Smiling, rubbing invisible crystals between her
fingers, she said that Egyptian priests abstained from salt
because they believed it increased sexual desire. Swim-
ming a bit closer, she said that the Romans referred to a
man who was in love as salax, which meant in a salted
state, and which, she added with a mischievous glint,
was the origin of the word salacious. In traditional Japa-
nese theater, before each performance, they used to scat-
ter salt onstage to protect the actors from evil spirits. In
Haiti, the only way to break a spell and bring a zombie
back to life was with salt. Until 1408, the French salted
their babies instead of baptizing them, and the Dutch
placed hunks of salt in their children's cribs, and the
Arabs protected their children by putting salt in their
hands on the eve of the seventh day after their birth.
Old Jews, as in the Book of Ezekiel, sprinkled babies
with salt to protect them from the evil eye. According
to the Shulchan Arukh, the book of Jewish laws, Jews
must touch salt only with their middle and ring fingers,
because if a Jew uses his thumb, his children will die,
and if a Jew uses his pinkie, he will become poor, and if a
Jew uses his index finger, he will become a murderer. For
Jews, salt was a pact, and a covenant, and a superstition,
and a punishment, and a downfall, and a cornerstone,

and a blessing, and a misfortune, and also a secret. She fell silent. I asked her what secret. I asked her how she knew so much about salt, but Tamara just smiled and told me that where we were was the lowest point on earth. Over there, she said, pointing to some tall yellowish rocks, is where some experts believe that Lot's wife, when she looked back to see the destruction of Sodom, turned into a pillar of salt. And over there, she said, signaling a huge plateau with her eyes, was the biblical fortification of Masada, where an entire population of Jews, rather than surrender to the Romans, committed mass suicide. Tamara took her hand out of the water and sucked a finger. And over there, she said, pointing her just-sucked finger at the mountains beyond the sea, is Jordan. I liked her long pale index finger better than the gray mountains of Jordan. Not far from us, somewhere in that same dead and salty sea, someone's prayer was already fading.

NO ONE LOOKS DOWN. That's what struck me on another trip, walking the gray streets of Warsaw on that first afternoon, dressed in a pink coat, still bleary, still wearing the same dirty wrinkled clothes—under that awful, garish pink coat—that I'd traveled from Guatemala in. No one greeted me. No one smiled at me. But no one looked down either. Men and women, young and old, they all turned to stare at me without any sort of judgment in their eyes, without emotion, without curiosity, maybe without even thinking me out of place in pink. As though for Poles looking down were a sign of cowardice. As though for Poles the last one to look down, the last one to blink, was declared winner of the game. But a critical game. An unrelenting game. A game between two blind pedestrians putting their lives on the line without realizing it.

It wasn't yet four o'clock in the afternoon, but night had fallen. I walked quickly, trying to warm up. I was underdressed or poorly dressed in that pink coat, and remembering that there's nothing lonelier than watching all the other passengers happily exit the airport and being the only one left standing there, at a still-revolving baggage carousel with not a single suitcase on it, recently landed in a country so foreign and frigid and feeling a nakedness that had nothing to do with clothes, those clothes that I—histrionic pink pedestrian in an abysmally gray city—was now missing and pining for and were lost in some corner of the world.

An airport official had helped me fill out a form. Then he stared at me gravely and told me in very poor English that they'd have the bag sent to my hotel. I began babbling that I'd be at that hotel for only one night, that the following day I'd be traveling by train—and here, mid-sentence, I cut myself off for a second while I measured my words, while I decided in that endless second whether or not to tell the official I'd

be traveling by train to Auschwitz; or perhaps while I
decided whether or not I'd go by train to Auschwitz,
to Block 11 of Auschwitz, where my grandfather had
been prisoner, in 1942. Although in part that was why
I'd come to Poland—to go to Auschwitz, to see the cell
in the basement of Block 11 where my grandfather had
been prisoner—the truth is, I didn't know if in the end
I'd board that train bound for the extermination camp
and the gas chambers and the crematorium and Block
11 and the cells in the basement where my grandfather
had been trained by a boxer, in 1942. I don't know why
I wasn't convinced I'd go. Fear of Auschwitz? Fear of
the word Auschwitz? Fear of traveling by train to Auschwitz? Fear of forming part of that mass of tourists
that goes to Auschwitz, that deplorable, sensationalist
mass of tourists that one could even say worships the
pornography of all things savage? In any case, and without saying something I shouldn't, fear of something.

The airport official was still staring at me steadily in
that never-ending second of silence, perhaps bewildered
or just waiting for me to finish my sentence. And so
I opened my mouth a little, as though to encourage
the words. But the words, capricious, insolent, wanted
no encouragement. I looked down. I slipped my hand
quickly into my pants pocket and felt the cold yellow slip
of paper and thought of my grandfather's hands, pale and
impeccable, drawing hats and playing with domino tiles.
My grandfather had been captured by Gestapo soldiers

in front of his house in Łódź, in November of 1939, as
he and his friends and his girlfriend played a game of
dominoes. He was sixteen years old. He then spent the
rest of the war—the next six years—as a prisoner in
various concentration camps, including Sachsenhausen,
and Neuengamme, and Buna Werke, and Auschwitz,
where a Polish boxer saved his life, training him to fight
not with his fists but with words. My grandfather left
Poland in 1945 and refused ever to return, refused ever to
pronounce another word in Polish. He lived out the rest
of his life in Guatemala, deeply offended by his coun-
trymen, and his native land, and his native tongue. The
Poles, he used to say to me, betrayed us. And so every
time I mentioned that I wanted to travel to Poland, that
I wanted to visit Łódź, my grandfather laughed bitterly
or stood and stormed off in a fury or spat a couple of
insults at me or perhaps at the entire Polish population.
But a few weeks before he died, by then weak, emaciated, and delirious (he thought there were Gestapo soldiers in his room, at his deathbed, waiting for him), my
grandfather wrote out his complete address for me on a
little sheet of yellow paper: ground floor of a building
on the corner of Zeromskiego Street and Persego Maja
Street, number 16, close to the Zielony Rynek market,
close to Poniatowskiego Park. Like a little yellow testa-
ment. Like a little clue to the family treasure. Like a
little inheritance left to a grandson. I took that yellow
paper from his trembling hand and folded it in two

and I knew immediately that my grandfather had given me much more than a wrinkled sheet of yellow paper. It was a mandate. An order. A dictate. An itinerary. A travel guide. A few coordinates on the mysterious and uneven map of our family. It was, in short, a prayer. His last prayer. There, on that folded yellow sheet of paper, with the last scrawl of his own hand, which I was now— standing in the Warsaw airport—clinging to like a talisman, were the coordinates of my grandfather's personal history, a history that in a way was also mine. In the end, our history is our only patrimony.

The Polish official was still staring at me steadily. I tried to smile at him, in order to regain some degree of calm or levity, in order not to feel so abandoned in the middle of Warsaw. But all that came out was a forced and awkward expression. The official, solemn, waited in silence, as though he knew I hadn't finished that faraway sentence about Auschwitz, as though he were giving me time to finish it and tell him what I had to tell him. And so I gathered my strength and clenched the yellow paper in my fist and stood tall and hastened to finish it.

The next day, I said, I was taking a train, heading south.

I sensed something bitter in my mouth. The taste, it occurred to me on the way out, of cowardice.

Bourekas. What? I asked. Bourekas, Tamara repeated, enunciating the three syllables slowly as she passed me the plastic bag. There are spinach ones and cheese ones, she said. My favorite breakfast, she added.

Behind us, the Citroën's door was open and the music on the radio was scarcely audible, like a continuous white purr or a gentle breeze. Tamara had also bought two coffees with milk and sugar, in cardboard cups—cold by now, of course, too weak and too sweet. But sitting there before a biblical sea, still barefoot and half-naked and half-dry and sharing a cigarette on a beach of salt and sand, I didn't care.

When we finished the bourekas and the coffee, Tamara began telling me about her job at Lufthansa. She told me that at first she'd thought of it as temporary, just until she found something better. She'd been there almost five years. It's not bad, she said. Pays well. I get to travel a lot. She smiled wryly, as if that were the handbook response. What about that man the other day, I asked, the one at the airport? Tamara reached for my cigarette and took a drag. Happens all the time, troublemakers, she said, and that was all she said. I asked her if anything like that had ever happened midair, during a flight. Nothing serious, she said, handing the cigarette back. But it occurred to me that maybe she wouldn't tell me. And then I kept thinking about planes. I smoked. The cigarette tasted like Tamara. Tamara tasted like salt. I watched her slowly turn and stretch out facedown, long and slender, her face now very close to my leg, her lips almost kissing my thigh. Sometimes, I said nervously, I dream I'm on a plane hijacked by Arab terrorists. I took another puff, watching her use a skilled hand to untie the bikini's red knot on her back. It's a recurrent dream, I said, exhaling. One of the Arab terrorists comes and stands in front of me, I said, and in a panic, I begin reciting the few words of Arabic I remember hearing from my Lebanese grandfather. Her freckled face turning toward me, Tamara looked up with her big blue eyes. Lajem bashin, and kibe naye, and lebne, and mujadara, which are all names of Arabic foods, but they're the only Arabic words I know. Tamara smiled faintly. Then the Arab terrorist sticks a gun in my face and screams at me to go to hell, screams that I look like a Jew, that I am a Jew, and shoves his gun even closer. I can feel the gun right here, on my forehead, I said to Tamara, and the Arab is about to shoot, about to fire a bullet into my head and kill me, and so I tell him no, he's mistaken, I'm not a Jew.

Tamara stopped smiling and held out her hand, requesting the last drag of the cigarette. I gazed at her ankles, her feet. I could feel the warmth of her breath on my thigh.

That's your recurrent dream? she asked, serious, crushing the butt into the sand. Sometimes there's a slight variation, I said. Like what kind of variation? Like, for example I tell the terrorist mabruk. It's an Arabic word my father uses a lot. It means congratulations. You say congratulations to a terrorist? Sometimes. Or sometimes I say shesh besh, which means six five. Shesh means six in Persian, and besh means five in Turkish. Shesh besh. Six five. That's what my Lebanese grandfather would shout when we played backgammon on a magnificent mother-of-pearl table that he'd brought from Damascus, back in the twenties, and he'd roll the dice, and get a six and a five, and he'd shout shesh besh.

We were silent a while, listening to the white noise of the radio, of the faintly rippling water, of a bird, melodious and magnificent and looking half lost in the immense blue sky. Listening to it, I recalled that Beethoven once said or might have said that his inspiration for the first four notes of his Fifth Symphony— perhaps the four most important notes in the history of music—had been birdsong.

Tamara breathed sweetly, rhythmically, perhaps dozing on her towel. I kept staring at the glistening sea until my vision blurred, and then suddenly, my eyes cloudy and tearful, I realized or thought I realized that there was something essential in those shared waters, something more than the saltpeter and the holiness and the tourists smeared with mud, something even lower than the lowest point of the earth and even more ambiguous than an imposing invisible wall in the sea, something between two countries, between two cultures held apart and brought together by water so dead and so salty and from which we all come and to which we all return, all salted in fire.

So, TAMARA GOADED ME, in your dream you deny being a Jew, you deny your roots, your tradition, your heritage, you deny everything to save yourself?

I dried my eyes with one hand. Tamara didn't notice. Hers were half-closed, maybe against the sun.

Yeah, I guess so, I said. You lie? Yes, I lie. Sort of cowardly, don't you think? Yes, maybe, sort of. And doesn't that bother you? she said, opening her eyes. What? Denying your Judaism, lying, passing yourself off as someone else just to save yourself. She was leaning on her elbows, her red bikini barely containing her breasts. I could almost make out the dark contour of her nipples. I glanced quickly toward the water. Why should it bother me? I murmured. It's only a dream, I said, and Tamara made a face, as if to say: Don't be a fool. Or as if to say: No dream is only a dream. Besides, I said, it's the same as a Jew passing himself off as someone else, disguising himself as someone else to escape the Nazis. Tamara didn't say anything. In my opinion, I continued with a barely perceptible smile, it's better to be a living liar than a dead Jew. It's not the same thing, Eduardo, she murmured, laying her head back down on the towel, possibly irritated. Her hair, damp and wild and graying slightly, brushed my thigh. I noted fleetingly that her bikini bottom was tucked between her buttocks, as if sucked in by her buttocks, and I felt my penis begin to stir.

THERE WAS A JEW IN GUATEMALA named Peter, I told Tamara, trying not to look at her white ass, but his name wasn't really Peter. He was a Polish Jew, a Jew from Polish Galicia named Yosef. He spent the war years in Poland, never leaving Poland, traveling freely through the towns and forests and mountains of Poland, living among the Nazis under a false name. Someone else's name. The name Peter Zsanowsky. He adopted a Polish identity and the Polish name of a lumberjack named Peter Zsanowsky, and masked, camouflaged, lying, he managed to save his life. In Guatemala, until the day he died, even on his tombstone, he always called himself Peter.

THE JEWISH GREAT-GRANDFATHER of a friend of mine, I told Tamara, trying not to look at her smooth round calves, managed to get out of Germany using identification papers he'd taken from a German soldier, a Nazi soldier whose last name was Neuman. He escaped, disguised as a German soldier whose last name was Neuman. He escaped, disguised as one of the German soldiers who wanted to kill him. He passed himself off as someone else and that was how he survived. When he made it to Argentina, he decided to keep the name, the name of his executioner and his savior. Neuman.

THE FAMILY OF POLISH WRITER Jerzy Kosin´ski, I told Tamara, trying not to look at the exposed side of her breast, escaped the Nazis by passing themselves off as a Catholic family. At the end of 1939, the family, still using the name Lewinkopf, fled Łódź, the city of my grandfather. In fact, the house of the Lewinkopfs (on Gdan´ska Street) was only a few blocks from where my grandfather lived (on Zeromskiego Street), and I have no trouble imagining young Jerzy Kosin´ski, still named Józef Lewinkopf, playing dominoes with my grandfather, or playing soccer with my grandfather, or playing hide-and-seek among the trees of Ponia-towskiego Park with my grandfather. The Lewinkopfs finally arrived in Dabrowa Rzeczycka, a country town in the south of Poland. They assumed the identity of a Catholic family whose last name was Kosin´ski. They rented an apartment. They hung crucifixes and pictures of the Virgin Mary on the wall, and let them gather dust and cobwebs so they wouldn't look new or recently hung. Young Jerzy went to church with his father every Sunday. He studied the catechism. He was an altar boy. He made his First Communion. He was careful never to pee outside, in front of his Catholic friends. And that's how he managed to save himself, pretending to be part of a Catholic family, disguised as an altar boy, and from then on—until the day he died fifty years later in a New York bathtub—using the last name Kosin´ski.

My Polish grandfather, while a prisoner in Block 11 of Auschwitz, I told Tamara, trying not to look at the mole on the curve of her lower back, met a Jewish prisoner they called Kazik, who was one of the men in charge of removing the bodies of those shot at the Black Wall. Gnadenschuss, my grandfather explained. A single shot to the back of the head. They called him Kazik, but his name was Kazimierz Piechowski, my grandfather told me. He was a Pole, from Tczew. He was the ankle guy—the one in charge of dragging all the fresh bodies from the Black Wall, one by one, by the ankles, to the Auschwitz crematorium. In June of 1942, together with three other prisoners, Kazik escaped through the main gate of Auschwitz, dressed as an SS second lieutenant, an Untersturmführer. In a stolen black uniform, a crisp uniform that hid his emaciated body and the number tattooed on his forearm (918), Kazik disguised himself as an Untersturmführer in the SS, shouted in German the orders that an Untersturmführer in the SS would shout, saw the guards immediately open the main gate of Auschwitz

(ARBEIT MACHT FREI), and disguised as his own enemy,
lying, managed to gain his freedom.

A FEW YEARS AGO, I told Tamara, trying not to look
at the slightly raised red mound between her thighs that
might have been the gentle rise of her warm vulva, I met
an old Polish Jew who had escaped the Nazis dressed as
a little Catholic girl.

Discreetly, I made a slight adjustment to my bathing suit.

He told me that one winter day, dressed as a girl, he'd
traveled with his parents to a monastery in the middle
of a forest, on the outskirts of Warsaw. It was snowing
that day in the forest and the monastery, in the snow,
amid snow-covered trees, looked enchanted and blue.
His parents handed him over to some Catholic nuns at
the monastery, along with a fake birth certificate and a
fake baptismal certificate, and said good-bye. He was
then five years old. He spent the rest of the war living in
that monastery on the outskirts of Warsaw, disguised as
a Catholic girl, dressed and groomed and made up like
a Catholic girl. With golden braids. In a skirt. Living
for years among Catholic girls. Kneeling and making
the sign of the cross and praying in Latin, along with all
the other Catholic girls.

I sat up a bit. I adjusted my bathing suit once again.

The first days or weeks at the monastery, he told me,

he'd kept his left hand closed tight, balled into a little
fist. The nuns tried to open it, to uncurl it, but he just
squeezed it harder, tighter, as though preparing to hit
someone. He ate like that and bathed like that and
prayed like that and even slept like that, with his left
hand balled into a little fist under the pillow. Just before
he'd arrived at the monastery, his father, kneeling in the
forest in the snow, had taken his left hand and had written there, on his palm, in black ink, his real name. His
boy name. His Hebrew name. His Jewish name. So he
wouldn't forget. So he could keep it secret. His father,
kneeling there, had named him in black ink between
the lines of his palm, in secret, in the middle of a forest,
on the outskirts of Warsaw. And as he was telling me
this, he raised his hand, I said to Tamara. He looked
like a witness swearing to tell the truth, I said. But after
days or weeks of living in the monastery, his real name
had already faded away.

Tamara opened her mouth slightly, perhaps to say
something or ask something, but I didn't let her.

I remember that the only time his voice trembled, I
said, was when he recited, in a benevolent tone, a tone
full of affection, the names of each of the nuns. He still
knew the names of each one of the fifteen or twenty
nuns who'd taken care of him. I also remember that he
described to me in detail the inside of that monastery
in the forest, I told Tamara, but I don't remember anything about his description. He might have described

the dark hallways and the ancient walls and the vaulted ceilings of the monastery. He might have described all the religious imagery in the monastery, and the hallways echoing constantly with Latin hymns. But I don't remember. I remember only his gaze. Because while he was describing it to me, he kept staring upward. An enigmatic, pious gaze, a frightened gaze. As if he could still see that monastery from the inside, or were still inside that monastery now. As if he'd never left that monastery in the forest, I said to Tamara, that monastery that had imprisoned him for years but had also saved his life. Because it was his gaze, I said, his fearful and almost childish gaze, that allowed me to imagine what he felt living there, imprisoned, captive not only to those dark damp walls but also to another language, other prayers, other clothing, another identity. And I was also able to imagine everything else. His parents letting his hair grow long enough to make two golden braids; dressing him in a pink dress and a girl's shoes; putting a touch of makeup on his lips and cheeks; writing his name on the palm of his hand; persuading him in Yiddish that his name was no longer that one, the one written in black ink on the palm of his hand, but Teresa or Natasza or Magdalena; his parents saying good-bye in front of the enormous door of the monastery in the snow, perhaps both covered in snow, perhaps knowing they would never see him again, perhaps weeping at the sight of that confused, pretty Catholic girl.

I paused, while with the fingernail of my index finger I scratched at tiny slivers of salt.

Of course he lost his parents, I went on, and he lost his childhood, his innocence, his name, his religion, his country, and even his manhood, but he saved himself, dressed as a Catholic girl for years in a monastery in the forest. He denied his Judaism and he denied his manhood and that's how he saved himself, I said to Tamara. Or who knows, I said, maybe his Judaism and his manhood were seized from him, and that's how he saved himself.

The only sound was the insistent scratching of my fingernail on the salt.

And that's the way it is, no? I said to Tamara, who was staring at me harshly, almost forlorn. Everyone decides how to save themselves, I said. Perhaps with a fundamentalist doctrine, or a series of fables and allegories, or a book of rules and norms and prohibitions, or the disguise of a lumberjack or a German soldier or a Catholic girl or an Orthodox Jew, or a cowardly lie told in a dream on a plane. With whatever it takes, whatever makes the most sense to us, whatever hurts the least. Tamara stared at me, more forlorn than ever. Though the truth is that they're lies, I said. And we all believe our own lie. We all cling to the name we believe suits us best. We all act out the role of our best disguise. But none of it matters. In the end, no one is saved.

I'd said it as if it were something definitive, or as

if I knew what I was talking about, or as if I really believed it.

I fell silent, staring out into space. I felt void. But void of words. Void of emotions. Void of color. Void of all that fulfills us or that we imagine fulfills us.

Suddenly, I felt a dull ache in my left hand. I hadn't realized that I'd been clenching it for some time, tightly, into a fist. But despite the pain, I didn't want to unclench it. Maybe out of a desire to keep up the macho pose. Maybe out of fear that on opening it I'd find there—written between the lines of my palm in black ink—my other name, my Hebrew name: Nissim. Eight days after I was born, as per Jewish tradition, and because Eduardo isn't a Hebrew name, my father named me Nissim. My Hebrew name, Nissim, means miracles. But seeing my clenched fist, it struck me that that name, my other name, my Jewish name, the name that my father had one day written in black ink on my tiny newborn palm, over time had also faded away.

Tamara raised a hand and held it out to me, perhaps just stretching, perhaps searching for my hand, perhaps in search of a cigarette that was no longer there, and let it drop onto my thigh. And she left her hand there. Warm, soft, immobile, palm up. As if it were any old object or as if it were not her own hand, but the hand of someone else. Another's hand. A foreign hand. A fragile hand, dry and warm and salt-stained.

So are you saved? I didn't understand her question.

Suddenly, her voice sounded distant, hoarse, velvety. Are you saved, on the plane, from the Arab terrorists? I looked down, searching for something. Are you saved, at the end of your dream? I looked for her back, her freckled shoulders, her wide hips, her round white ass almost naked and covered in tiny translucent hairs. Her hand lay motionless on my thigh. In the distance, the mountains of Jordan stood gray and still.

About the Author

Eduardo Halfon was born in Guatemala City, moved to the United States at the age of ten, went to school in South Florida, studied Industrial Engineering at North Carolina State University, and then returned to Guatemala to teach literature for eight years at Universidad Francisco Marroquín. Named one of the best young Latin American writers by the Hay Festival of Bogotá, he is also the recipient of a Guggenheim Fellowship and the prestigious José María de Pereda Prize for the Short Novel. He has published eleven previous books of fiction in Spanish. *The Polish Boxer*, his first book to appear in English, was a *New York Times* Editor's Choice selection and finalist for the International Latino Book Award. Halfon currently lives in Nebraska and frequently travels to Guatemala.

The Translators

Lisa Dillman translates from Spanish and Catalan and teaches in the Department of Spanish and Portuguese at Emory University in Atlanta, Georgia. She has translated numerous books by Spanish and Latin American writers including Andrés Barba, Christopher Domínguez Michael, Sabina Berman, and Juan Filloy.

Daniel Hahn is a writer, editor, and translator with some forty books to his name. His translations from Portuguese, Spanish, and French include fiction from Europe, Africa, and the Americas, and nonfiction by writers ranging from Portuguese Nobel laureate José Saramago to Brazilian footballer Pelé. He is also the editor of the new *Oxford Companion to Children's Literature*. He lives in Brighton, England.

BELLEVUE LITERARY PRESS is devoted to publishing
literary fiction and nonfiction at the intersection of
the arts and sciences because we believe that science
and the humanities are natural companions for
understanding the human experience. With each book
we publish, our goal is to foster a rich, interdisciplinary
dialogue that will forge new tools for thinking
and engaging with the world.

To support our press and its mission, and for our full
catalogue of published titles, please visit us at blpress.org.

BELLEVUE LITERARY PRESS
New York